FIVE
WINDOWS

FIVE WINDOWS

A NOVEL

JON ROEMER

DZANC
BOOKS

5220 Dexter Ann Arbor Rd.
Ann Arbor, MI 48103
www.dzancbooks.org

Library of Congress Cataloging-in-Publication Data

Names: Roemer, Jon, 1964- author.
Title: Five windows / by Jon Roemer.
Description: Ann Arbor, MI : Dzanc Books, [2019]
Identifiers: LCCN 2019013631 | ISBN 9781945814945
Subjects: | GSAFD: Suspense fiction.
Classification: LCC PS3618.O3724 F58 2019 | DDC 813/.6--dc23
LC record available at https://lccn.loc.gov/2019013631

First US edition: September 2019
Interior design by Michelle Dotter

Printed in the United States of America

10   9   8   7   6   5   4   3   2   1

CHAPTER ONE

I DON'T KNOW THEIR names, and I'm not looking for anyone, but now and then, it's worth a look out the windows at the city and the skyline and the leather-soled rabble on the sidewalks below.

We're on one of the hills, and only partway up, so if they've climbed this far, it's a good place to pause and take stock. Just a block down the hill, past the flowered trees and pretty covings, it's miserably busy. Monster commuter lanes are crammed and heaving. But here the steepness slows things. Traffic is at a minimum. People notice each other, heading down, climbing up, passing through our little crossroads to places less quiet.

Across the hill's slope, three cottages squat side by side like burly brothers—one blue, one pink, one green. Ugly gray smoke streams from their front windows, a thick blanket that covers the first signs of flames. Every day the three of them sit shoulder to shoulder, looking out over the city, unmoved by what they're seeing, indifferent, unimpressed—until early this morning, when something must've snapped, something must've shifted, and they started to cook from the inside out. Now, together, they're going up in flames, burning into each other and, just so quickly, threatening the rest of the hill and the hundreds of houses packed close as family—contiguous brittle kindling.

From my windows, I can see pump and ladder trucks arriving, firemen scrambling with hatchets and hoses then straddling the peaks of the surrounding roofs. They work in a patterned way, with a practiced approach that seems too slow and shorthanded. Helicopters and tanker planes should be dumping retardants. The streets should be running orange with special chemical stuff.

But their expertise is breathtaking, controlling the burn carefully, guiding it off a small family bungalow toward another where an old couple lives, just to keep a dozen others from falling to cinders. They lead it around a chimney then onto a neighbor's roof, a steep slope of shingles arranged in brown and red zigzags that turn terminally black in a furious flash—all efforts keep it from taking the entire hillside. But then the smoke rushes toward me, dark and obscure.

Right below me on the sidewalk, a woman is whistling a gritty trap tune, wearing headphones the size of pineapples and a stiff orange vest. Through the smoke, she is blocking off the street, setting up cones and sawhorses as she wails through the chorus, flubbing the lyrics—really wrecking the refrain, not anywhere close. A young man in long shorts headbangs along with her as he pushes a stroller to the far curb. An office worker stands in his way there, pretty much frozen, baffled by the smoke and the street barriers, desperate for someone tell him what to do.

"Shelter in place, sir," the woman shouts up at me. "Need to keep the streets clear for emergency vehicles."

"Is everyone okay? Do you know what happened?" I shout.

"There's been a fire, sir. We're trying to limit looky-loos."

"Of course." I have to cough against the smoke. "But do you know what caused it? Is it safe to stay here?" Sirens are still going, and ash has started falling, floating like it's looking for somewhere to go. "Is there anything I should do?" I'd like to know if I should get down there and run around my building, taking aim with the garage hose.

Where is everyone, anyway? The neighbors' windows are empty, and I see no rush of blankets and casseroles. No signs of concern for the family—the *three* families—losing their homes today.

"Sir, please," the woman says. She toes her traffic cones, trying for clean lines, and with a shift in the wind, my view clears again. The smoke and ash are redirected, and I can watch the fire start to calm, contained to the three houses. The extra engines and their equipment are beginning to pull away. Within the hour, the structures are doused and dripping, leaving a charred jagged scar on the side of our hill. And then it's over. Just like that. The street below is opened again, and the crews and their gear go back at their stations, leaving us alone and on the lookout.

Blue tarps dot the neighborhood, marking two close calls not so long ago. That's how combustible this place has become, and in the days that follow, rumors run wild. Christmas candles. Insurance scams. Arsonist radicals. Today I read terrible stories fingering a pair of locals hurling gas-soaked rags, and by nightfall I see sirens charging up the hill to an encampment in the park where the suspects are supposed to be settled.

The fire was thrilling. I have to admit that. Especially the smoke coming at me like it did. There is something upending, something root-deep unruly, just under the surface here. A fiery splendor to leave you destroyed and renewed.

I never shared this with Sylvie, even when we were together. Here, in a place like this, there's plenty already. Disruption is a lifestyle, the word of the day every day. It's not something to brag on. It's a given and a starting point. And as much as we felt it—and lived it and yelled it—we couldn't make a go of it. This place never worked for us.

Instead, a lot of silence, a lot of doors slamming, and a lot of hours avoiding each other. She was big in tech retail. I was getting a small publishing house off the ground, with a program devoted to the unexpectedly overlooked. We met through friends just after college and had ten good years before the last two got ugly. Now, seven years gone, we both want better for each other—probably, finally, if she ever gives it much thought anymore.

"You think things you're not telling me," Sylvie liked to yell at me. "Plans…ideas…goals you're keeping secret, that I don't even know about." She'd talk real fast and point right at me. "Something's rotten at the heart of you. You're steering things in directions I know nothing about."

That's how she saw it, how she interpreted my general feeling, my unspoken belief that our basics weren't good. Our fights escalated fast and ended abruptly, as quick as the bedroom door could slam. "Everybody has ideas," I liked to yell back. "And I can't yell everything that comes into my head."

Two years of suspicions and accusations. When she left, she dropped a loaded note on my desk: "Enjoy your fucking view." I've had it framed and set on the sill beside my desk, which sits in sunshine before a San Francisco panorama, a windowed perch that will always once have been Sylvie's too.

Our divorce was a buyout, as everything is here. She left me our apartment, along with a trust providing enough income to keep me afloat. A minor role reversal, and when it happened, it felt about right, laid out on a ledger with a few tidy columns showing which way the money would flow.

I gutted the apartment after she left, front to back, ripping out the ceiling and walls, aiming for something loft-like, one long open space from the bay windows on the street to the kitchen in the back. The only real furniture floats in the middle: a bed, bookshelves, a couch, and a single low-slung chair. My desk, a rat's nest of papers and computer screens, sits beside five tall windows at the front. All the walls are gone, the studs exposed along with the conduits and the plumbing. I wanted an industrial feel—unpolished, uncovered. Some days it feels like I started remodeling but never got past the demolition. Other days, I don't miss the slamming doors.

The folks upstairs had to live through the teardown. Before things got started, I knocked and delivered a note with the schedule. "I've talked to the contractor. We'll try to stick to nine to five, so you'll be at work while most of the noise is happening." I was standing in our vestibule, where our front doors both open. I remember grinning, and apologizing for grinning. I was so excited to get things going. But Ken kept it brief. He took my note. He tried smiling. He nodded and assured me it wouldn't be a problem. "It's fine, it's fine," he said, quick as he could, then he shot a look behind him and closed the door fast.

It's a couple that lives up there. I've admired them from a distance. It's been maybe eight years since the two men bought the unit, coming and going almost always together, almost always with arms around waists or shoulders. They are demonstrative in easy unselfconscious ways, one black, one white, both handsome and thin, ready with a wave from inside their love bubble. I like what I see there. It isn't faked or saccharine or put on for appearances. There's even something subversive about their hand-holding, their closeness in public. Even here, at this late date, there's something slightly radical about two men so open, so totally uninhibited. We can all take something good from that.

I also love them for their fighting. I can hear them go at it, even down at my desk, shouting and arguing, usually very late at night. Their voices are too similar to parse out the details, which one is the aggressor and who might need backup. But they go at it like dogs or two brothers who know precisely which words cut deep.

From what I can tell it's usually over a bad repair or an iffy paint color. Little stuff, domestic stuff. When it happens too often, two or three times in a week, it can seem like it's dangerous. Those days, I've worried. I've thought about knocking, sticking my nose in. There's the pounding down the stairs, the slamming of the front door—that happens now and then, but not really so regularly. Which is another reason I like seeing them together, shoulder to shoulder, one arm over the other, two humans trying to get along, finding their way back to their love balloon. You can label it as you'd like, but they genuinely seem the better for it. The safety of their coupledom, restored and returned to after they've ripped the flesh off. A regular upending, a habitual recasting. Sylvie and I never figured that out.

The morning after the three-house fire, there's still the smell of burnt timber and melted plastic. The odor that lingers is unsettling. And with the dampness in the fog, the ash has turned to grit, painting cars and trash bins with a light gray film. Together, collectively, the whole hillside is feeling it, interrupting stroller walks and regular tooth brushing, everyone leaning in and listening for sirens behind the next fire truck.

Several blocks off, I can see the scorched frames still waiting for tarp protection, crammed like a pricey kaleidoscope, the stubby earthquake shacks, the skinny, tall Edwardians, the oversized picture windows that came with botched remodels, and the glass and steel structures built on teardowns and tech cash. This last one in particular, it's like a semi-invisible hand holding a very thick wallet, marking the streets and claiming prime spots.

Across the street is a sudden colony of women. I watched the building fill after two years of reworking. Three stories of Edwardian trim and bay windows have been tidied and balanced, shedding their old chipped and faded look. Now it's adorned with classy down-lighting, stately mailboxes, and a modern-but-understated security gate replacing the one that used to swing in the wind.

There used to be plywood on more than one window, and from across the street, I watched six families' evictions, a pitiless train of unmarked vans and stuffed sedan trunks. It took nine months to redirect those particular futures. Two sets of young parents with kids, a young couple without kids, two elderly couples, and one taking care of a trouble-making boy. Near the end, that young boy posted a scrawled sign in his window, a piece of notebook paper taped in place, illegible even from across the street. For a while before that, he was on the corner most evenings, trying to drum up a dealing business, hands deep in his pockets as he paced. I never saw any transactions go down, but I never knew how much he'd need, the number of drive-bys, to make a go of it. The elderly couple he lived with was the last to leave. When their day came, a middle-aged man, shirtless, tattooed, with a real sketchy vibe, carted them away in a shiny Range Rover.

After that, things moved quickly, and everything was new there, a testament to how people shape the world for themselves. Plenty of others nearby have been spruced up—gone condo, switched out families—but a turning point came with that young boy's departure. His removal. His extraction. Depends on what you're thinking. But in the weeks that followed, there was a collective exhale. More runners, more dogs walkers. I now regularly see a very expensive stroller left parked on that corner for close to an hour.

From across the street, I watched new insides arrive: a white mountain of marble, a green river of glass tile, and a shrink-wrapped pallet of fixtures and hardware. New wood-framed windows replaced the ones gone crooked. Two separate power washes cleared a century of cobwebs, followed by tasteful coats of shaded grays and whites. When it finally looked perfectly refreshed but still perfectly old, open houses were announced and vigorously attended. In the space of a few weeks, while still conspicuously empty, six new couples, all women, stood out front with their arms crossed, staring hard from the eaves to the street.

I watched and I watched, and the women undoubtedly saw me watching. They probably heard me, too, groaning over end tables and high-end delivery trucks. They draped bed sheets on their windows before their custom shades arrived—a group message. *That's enough. Show's over. Enjoy your fucking view.*

I waved down from my window and tried greeting a young couple. "Hello!" I shouted. "Welcome!" I said. Just trying to brighten their moving day.

They both turned and looked up, confused and a little concerned. I got a quick wave back before they leaned into each other and went back to supervising the couches and bed frames hoisted over their sidewalk, a parade of tasteful patterned upholstery disappearing through the sleek gate.

Honestly, genuinely, I'm happy to have them, to have new neighbors that notice and respond to me—at least more than the mothers who used to come and go, always letting their children loose and tolerating the dealer kid. Their leaving—their booting—was tough to watch. I got emotional. It made me angry, every time, and I feel helpless to this day. Especially because I don't know where they went. How far they had to move, and if that messed with their jobs, if it screwed up their marriages, if their kids got settled in other, better schools. But there's also another thought: we never really clicked, never shared much in passing; we never really found our neighbor groove. Frankly, seriously, they didn't seem to like me—they weren't so friendly, giving me the stink eye and never much else. The kid working the street corner never earned their attention either. To my knowledge, none of them confronted him or called the police. For years, they watched me and I watched them, and for all kinds of reasons, none of them so beautiful, I'm the one who's still here, looking down on pricey strollers and watching these fancy women move in their stuff.

Professionals, high-income—white, Asian, and Latina. Half moved in alone, half arrived as couples. No children in sight, and apparently they feel safe here. My peering is their most immediate threat. Just a few weeks ago, someone finally waved to me, quickly but friendly-like, before pulling her new linen blinds tight.

"What about you?" one of my neighbors grilled me, a bespectacled senior I'd never seen on my street. "This is no place for beginners." We were both at a meeting in the library basement: a public presentation by an Afghan scholar, a specialist in global poverty and First World waste, invited that night to walk us through the numbers, the horrors at our doorsteps, what we walk past daily and must surely be numb to—an hour-long scolding that included a head count of people just trying to get a roof over their head and the magnitude of our shameful disregard. A powerful encounter—not my last in that basement—witnessing the disgust on that visiting scholar's face. Also notable was her visible distraction, how she couldn't stop staring at the setup in the corner, the library's commendable cookie buffet, a regular, modest, and locally sourced spread that occupies its own table and can be counted on to fill one or two extra seats.

My neighbor was clearly moved, enough to confront me. I'd watched her cross the room with very clear intentions, sussing me out, to identify my claim, to pinpoint when I had moved into her neighborhood and what I was doing in her local library basement. "We're a long way from Fisherman's Wharf."

"Totally agree," I told her. "Nineteen years and counting for me."

She took a step a closer to get a better look. "That's a start," she told me, and I smiled and nodded, happy to show her any and all deference. That was why I was there, what library basements are for: richer encounters than quick nods on the sidewalk, more intimate

examinations than the frozen pizza aisle allows. We were both probably amped from the presentation we'd just heard. That's probably
why things went south like they did.

"You're that guy," she told me then, suddenly struck by how she
knew me. "You're the guy in the window always pacing and ranting."

She was smallish, in layered knits, and seemed to live at a remove
behind thick eyeglasses. She was also close enough to reach up and
point a finger at my head.

"Are you okay?" she pressed me. "I mean, generally. Mentally.
You seem to spend a lot of time up there by yourself."

I smiled again, deferring again, like she must be ribbing me,
but when I took a quick look past her, no one else was smiling. A
small crowd was watching, mostly seniors holding punch cups and
a few scruffy young girls newly engaged by a community spirit and
no doubt surprised by the generous cookie spread. I felt trapped and
cornered; I didn't know this woman. She wasn't someone I'd seen on
the sidewalks in front of mine, and she wasn't one of the new arrivals across the street. But she wasn't budging, her expression wasn't
changing, and up close, her lenses were kind of filthy. She was dead
serious, and she was waiting for me to explain myself.

I did my best to reassure her. "My work keeps me captive. Slave
to my job. Chained to my desk. Maybe you know what it's like to run
your own business…"

"No," she said. "No, I don't." And she kept it to that, unmoving,
staring me down, waiting for something more reasonable or exculpa-
tory. On her breath, too much coffee, and on her chin, the crumbs
of lemon bars. As we stood there, her mood turned, and she seemed
deeply perturbed, as if she were due an apology, or a flat-out confes-
sion, a few incriminating words she already had in mind, self-damn-
ing ones that would prompt her to scold me, maybe poke me on the
shoulder. Which she did anyway with her pointy finger bone.

"Well, you have to really love it," I tried and took a step back.

I wasn't used to getting poked, especially for something like that: spending time working, sticking close to my chair. Her complaint was that I was too often at my desk. I would think that showed fortitude, a sign of being serious. You must be a good egg if you really love your work.

But this woman shrugged back at me, in a mean way, in a mocking way, and she seemed perfectly comfortable walking off with her conclusions, dropping her plate with its lemon bar smears in the cookie buffet's recycling bin.

"Have a nice day," I shouted after her, which was a mistake, echoing through the library basement. Most of the crowd heard me. The meeting was over; they were still watching us. Together, they leaned in and gave me a hard look.

I don't always love it, my perch with my view, my little office set up. My job—reviewing manuscripts, putting books together—it's routed with filth and violent fantasies, revenge stories, monster stories, and stories of survivors who aren't so sympathetic. That's what I do all day. I sludge through submissions where the essential trend is downward, toward the messy expansion of acceptable levels of violence. But a quick look at the pretty view, and I'm ready to keep going, I can get back to it. I suppose it's enabling, in its own picturesque, fire-scarred way.

What makes it worthwhile is the buried gem, the radically exceptional. That is what drives and pushes me daily, keeps me chained to my desk. I start each day with the light from my window and the search for the unexpectedly overlooked.

But mostly, generally, it's the opposite of all that. Most days it's like standing in the middle of a dark current, the kind that comes with major flooding, a steady flow of random bits torn off from other bits. Too-private confessions, paper-thin entertainments, philosophical examinations that read slow and dry. Every day I read what people are thinking and have taken the time to detail and organize, time alone at a keyboard, not posting, not watching, stories people think worth sharing, that others should be hearing. Dozens by the day, hundreds by the week, and mostly, it's disturbing, this constant need to be heard.

My little publishing startup produces ten books a year. I wade through many times that by the end of each month. Most of it gets done at my desk, alone, where I pace and rant aloud to myself, apparently in plain sight and with enough flourish that people outside seem to notice.

"You really have to love it," I said to an older gentleman not a minute later while still getting tough looks in that library basement. He was also in layered knits, but he was even more demanding, even more in my face. He'd obviously seen the old woman leave disgusted, and when I shrugged at him too, his face turned dark. He even gave me a little shove, before following her off past the snacks and periodicals.

"What the hell…" I said, this time under my breath. I don't think I'd ever been shoved before, not so deliberately, and I've learned now I'm not the type to shove back.

I keep my nose down. I work long hours. I'm not used to anyone thinking of me as a threat. I often wish I could explain how I spend my days, what I'm up to when I'm sitting in my five tall windows. I wish I could put it on a sign around my neck. Or scrawl it on paper and tape it to the glass.

"Enjoy your fucking view," the old man scolded me, and I still don't know what I did to set them off.

This morning out my window, a half-dozen Frenchmen are climbing the hill, bantering, laughing, arm in arm with wine and baguettes, headed to the park several blocks up. They are unexpected.

We don't get a lot of tourists. You have to know where you're going to end up here. One of them points his camera up at me. It's a classic old Canon with a worn leather case and a thin leather strap. He takes a shot and watches me while he lowers it, working the lever, advancing the film. It must be a weird snapshot, me looking down at him. And it's followed by nothing: there's no wave or smile, no howdy, no *bonjour*. As if I weren't looking straight down his shutter.

He jogs to join the others, who have stopped to wait for him. They turn to look at what he's photographed. From the handful of them: not a nod, not a single *allo*. They turn back to the hill, each gripping another's shoulder, not bothered at all by the smell of everything that's been on fire this morning.

CHAPTER TWO

THIS MORNING, IT'S A tell-all by an assistant to a Twitter star. That's how she's pitched it, but it's a standard memoir, really, about growing up in Haiti, then her undergrad at Columbia, then her brief modeling career in LA, before signing up to serve as a more successful model's clever and wise online surrogate. It's an exploration of everything that's made her the woman she is today—the voice of someone else—but with entrée to the elite and a diet of cocktails no one can pronounce. It's worth a look, worth moving to my Saved queue, if only because it's so out of our ordinary.

We shy away from Twitter stars—and TV stars and movie stars, anything with a short expiration date. Instead we go for the unconventionally thoughtful. Books you don't expect to love but that still pull you close to a bookstore shelf. First-person stories by skyscraper window washers. A darkly comic novel about a small town's unraveling. A portrait of the lifecycle of Amazon cardboard. Each is nicely grounded while stretching far and wide.

This is the first line of the Twitter assistant's book: "You don't know me but I'm kind of a big deal. A bigger deal than anyone you probably know." Right away I worry about the tone. That much swagger won't hold for a couple hundred pages. And then there's the author photo, conspicuously included, which makes my heart sink.

Full color, in tight braids, with her smooth shoulders bared—and a puppy, a little puppy in a pink cowboy hat, held up close to her perfectly airbrushed face.

It's too much—too close to home, really. Almost as if she's mocking us. Peering back from the photo, through their puppy-dog eyes, she's signaling she knows what we're really all about.

Puppies are our company secret. Our original sin. Everything we do, every marvelous book we unearth and present, is on the backs of puppies in tiny hats and precious outfits. Every one of us—all four of us in our tightly knit operation—is proud of our output, our boast-worthy projects, despite the hidden fact that everything is funded by obscenely large earnings from puppies on calendars in outlandish poses. Puppies in football gear, puppies in tutus, puppies dressed up for House of Windsor weddings. Puppies driving cars, playing golf, buying groceries. All photographed in scaled settings to match. Up-dated annually, a task I've always outsourced. A glossy, embarrassing, twelve-uddered cash cow that allows us to be as serious and thought-ful as we otherwise want.

It's not worth going on about. It's not something I'm proud of. Few people know; the connection is discreet, buried inside a fancy LLC. Mostly, it detracts from our main objective. Adorable puppies in exceptionally funny outfits have nothing to do with the books we produce.

Aside from feeding us cash, they're an innocuous frivolity, they're not good for our business, and an author photo like this one puts me on edge. So I delete the Twitter assistant from the Saved queue. It's a close call and a hard no. Maybe I'm acting rash, dismissing it too quickly—but enough with the puppies. I look out the window and try to reset myself.

On my screen, in the queue, a layman's survey of underwater engineering, a compendium of movable structures just under the oceans' surface, ones that will keep rising waters from destroying a lot of cities. A survival guide to the new hostile tides. It's intriguing. I'm into it. I'm ready to settle in, but something loud is going on behind me, heavy footsteps pounding down from the unit upstairs. Somebody running in a panic. I can't quite decipher it, but it sounds like someone swearing, someone horrified. Unusual this early in the day.

Then he's pounding on my door. I open it to Kenny, the thin white guy from upstairs. Terror full across his face. "I need help," he tells me. He's trying to stay composed, trying not to lose his breath, and also trying not to frighten me. "An ambulance. Call 911. Please."

I spot blood on his sleeve, then on his neck, his collar, the back of his head. He follows my look and swallows hard. "It's okay. I'm okay. I would drive him myself, but an ambulance would really help."

"Of course, of course." I'm fumbling for my phone. I'm an idiot for staring, for even pausing for a second. The only visitors I get are food deliveries and repairmen. I step out of the doorway, mortified to be blocking it, and wave him in while I struggle with the keypad.

"Just 911." He stays in our vestibule, wiping his shoes on the mat, but we both see the blood he's left there too. Then he grabs the doorframe, obviously looking for support, and lowers his head, focusing on his breath while I stand watching and on hold.

In my doorway, he's trying to get a grip on his situation. From the heave of his shoulders and the way his head is shaking, it's clear he can't believe it, that he finds himself there, first thing in the morning, at the end of someone's rope, a rope that clearly doesn't feel like his. He looks like a man literally framed by a situation he only now realizes he walked into. Then some shouting from upstairs, which is suddenly too familiar. He looks at me like I can't know what he's thinking—or he'd like to believe I haven't heard them before.

"Darrel had an accident. He's been doing some carving. He just wasn't being careful." He clearly wants to convince me, and I must look like I need it.

I nod to reassure him. "Of course," I tell him and tell the operator the same, explaining that someone's been cut and there appears to be bleeding.

The operator asks me, "Is everyone safe? Are you safe, sir?"

Kenny can hear her. He starts shaking his head, then nodding vigorously.

"Yes, yes," I tell her. "We would drive him in, but there is a lot of bleeding. A lot."

Help is on its way—I've at least contributed that much—but Kenny still stands there, panting in the vestibule. He stays against the doorframe for quite a long stretch, really, head bowed and shaking slowly, before he starts back up.

He gives the stairs a long look, saying something very quietly. The whole time I am wordless, just fixed on him and trying to figure out if all the blood really belongs to Darrel. I'm not finding the words to ask him straight out. I'm not at all sure about my place in this, as a neighbor, as an acquaintance, as someone who lives downstairs just sitting down to work.

Because in this heated minute, I'm preoccupied with my presumptions. And whatever is in my head starts to sync with Kenny's breathing. I have no real place or role in this. None of this is my doing or my problem or my issue. As he starts to hurry back up, I remember Darrel is up there, hurting, bleeding.

"It's okay. I'm taking care of it," I hear Kenny yelling.

He's left his door open. I've left mine open too, but suddenly I'm alone, left to wait for the ambulance, not sure if I should be going up to help. Panic like Kenny's, especially at the front door, is infectious. So I look for reassurance in what I know about Darrel.

It's not much, and it's uncomfortable, and I really don't like this kind of fishing, especially while sirens are starting up somewhere. I remind myself of my guiding principle, the idea of dimensional doubt—a familiar concept but a term I just now invented, a second after Kenny left my door—and by which I believe this: we can't know folks in their fullest, from all and every side, both backward and forward, and especially not as they know themselves, as their histories have shaped their own self-awareness. And we should react accordingly. Basically, I try not to put words in others' mouths and assign as few motives as possible. Minimal judgments. Restrained accusations. An avoidance of anything that smells of easy prejudice. I say this to myself as spilled blood darkens my doormat.

With the ambulance come police, a pair rushing upstairs then back down again. They see me in my doorway. The lights on their car flash in the street. They ask if they can come in, so I'm cornered while Darrel is taken out to the ambulance. Didn't even see a stretcher or how bad he looked.

I tell the officers all I know, from the couple's occasional yelling to their public hugging. "Totally harmless. I have no reason to believe they'd actually hurt each other."

"Got it," one says, scratching something on his notepad, the old-fashioned flip kind with wire binding along the top.

"You live alone?" the other asks, a midcareer man who doesn't look at me. He appears exhausted despite the early hour.

"I do now. Yes."

"For how long?" he asks, looking around the open stretch of my apartment, settling for a second on the windows' bright view.

"Seven years now."

"Seven years?" he says. The answer seems to trouble him. They look at one another then make their way out.

Outside, I can see Kenny sitting in the back of the ambulance, still bloodied under the lights, next to an EMT working hard on Darrel, who's probably stretched out between them, out of my view. They speed away and only turn the siren on several blocks off.

Then quiet resumes. It falls kind of heavy. I try to get back to oceanic engineering but end up in the vestibule, seeing Kenny's door still open. I look up Kenny's stairs, hear no one around, feel tempted to go up...but close it in front of me.

I try to work again, but my head isn't in it, and the sidewalks below are disturbingly empty. I'd rather figure out what happened and how they're both doing. Darrel and I, for whatever reason, have rarely spoken. All I know about him is what Kenny has told me. Kenny and I also haven't talked much, apart from a discussion about replacing the front light, and the concern we both had for a new transit hub nearby.

The police had come once before, that time late at night, after one of their shouting matches. But that night Kenny was outside waiting for them, standing with his hands in his pockets in the middle of the street. He'd flagged them down and talked to them curbside. It was obvious Kenny had called them himself. I got out of bed but stayed in the dark, a step or two back, watching Kenny point up at his unit above mine. I don't think the police went up. They drove off fairly quickly. False alarm. Dimensional doubt. Kenny ended up steering them clear. But before he headed back up, he waved at me briefly. I'd thought I was hidden.

"Do you have a minute?" he asked me that next morning, handing me a coffee outside our garage. I'm not usually out so early, but I was curious about the view from the street to my apartment. Just how much could someone see from everywhere else.

"I should apologize," Kenny told me. "I know we probably woke you." And then he told me he should explain more about Darrel. He knew their arguments had started to worry me. I wanted to disagree, but he started in first.

Darrel was younger than both Kenny and me, but he'd been around the block and had a tough go. This was his second time trying to set roots in San Francisco, returning after his husband died from a heart attack, in the living room of a condo they shared outside Dallas.

There in our driveway, Kenny rattled through the details. "Darrel and his husband were in love. Married ten years. They met here but escaped to something more affordable, where his husband could retire and they could live well." Kenny rolled his eyes at the idea of Dallas. "But after his death, his husband's sister, a pretty mean evangelical, contested the estate and ended up with a big chunk of it. That's when Darrel realized Dallas was no good. They'd been too insular, anyway. After his husband was gone, he had no social network, and the in-laws were circling like wolves."

I wasn't sure what to say. "You can't go home again." But that wasn't right, and I wished I had stopped him before he told me all this. It felt like Kenny was tattling or gossiping, and it felt like he thought I wanted to hear it. But I didn't. I don't need Darrel's biography. None of these details really matter to me. I will still call an ambulance whenever Kenny tells me, and I'm not lacking in sympathy for two people who need to yell.

Kenny shook his head. "Once you leave *this* town, there's no coming back."

I got what he meant. I understood that much. It's pricey here, it's not an easy town to live in—I'd witnessed an entire building get evicted. Complaining about the city is a common pastime, and when Kenny brought it up, it felt like a better way to cement our friendship. Instead of calling out Darrel, we could settle on something bigger, on terms we both shared. But Kenny quickly circled back. Darrel's story wasn't over. "He's had a tough go. He's had some good years, but not so many."

He stepped closer. He looked up at our windows, then lowered his voice. It hadn't occurred to me that Darrel could be listening, and I wished we could go back to carping on the city, the rising price of burritos, the quickening pace of new developments, the parking of strollers on troubled corners. "A real rough story," he went on, even as I tried not to look up. "His family fell apart in junior high. That was in Modesto, before he came to San Francisco. Before he came out, before he met his husband. He was sleeping at friends' houses and at his sister's, when his dad wasn't there. Both his mom and dad, the biological ones, were into some hard drugs and threw him out when they caught him with another kid on the block."

It was really too much. I didn't feel right: Darrel should be sharing this, not Kenny, and I was finally ready to tell him to stop. But then I realized how I didn't think of Darrel, how I never thought about him in terms of *race*. Together, they didn't seem to ask for it— he and Kenny, in their love bubble, seemed way beyond that, above that kind of trouble, or at least protected inside their bubble.

"Things got slightly better in high school," Kenny continued. "Darrel was a decent track star, and when his teammates caught on, one of their families took him in. I think they finally adopted him— like formally, legally—sometime in his late teens. So he had a few stable years with some normal family life."

"That is…a lot," I told him, as a way to land an answer. It was a lot to live through, a lot of hurdles to push past—and a lot to take in on our condos' sidewalk. And by then, as it sunk in, it felt less like loose chitchat and more like a defense, like a tightly wound argument, like a case for Darrel had to be made. As if Kenny had shared it because it was a big deal, bigger than both of us, and except for a little attitude about living in Dallas, he'd described his boyfriend within a well-reasoned framework, in a fairly detached analysis that somehow also felt intimate and intense.

I tried to nod along and dial back my discomfort, but then Darrel opened a window directly above us. He didn't lean out or say anything. He just perched there, sort of out of view but still letting us know he was there, watching, maybe listening. Kenny signaled he needed to go back upstairs, and before I left, I got a sense of the different views from the sidewalk, the angles, the perspectives, how someone could spot Darrel in his place or me at my desk.

Hours later, a car pulls up and Kenny is alone when he steps to the curb. He waves from below and talks up at me. "Darrel will be in the hospital for a while," he reports, then he sort of snorts and shrugs, obviously exhausted and uncomfortable having to report back to me. He's still spotted with dried blood.

I offer to bring in mail, pick up packages, whatever's helpful. Kenny thanks me and offers another plan instead, suggesting we meet up at the next library gathering, to review and respond to the new transit hub. It feels deeply trivial, way too inconsequential, especially with Darrel in a hospital bed. But I understand Kenny's need to normalize, to plan for something ordinary, to look ahead to events that won't involve blood.

I watch him hop across the sidewalk. He's carrying his blood-splattered shoes, so it's like he's tiptoeing, to compensate for the disruption, and I find myself drawn back to ocean-floor building, the lengths we have to go to save coastal cities. This quickly feels pretty trivial, too, with some hospital somewhere holding Darrel right now—but then I'm grateful to put my head down and lean into it.

About an hour later, I see a burly man in biker leather on the sidewalk below. Classic Tom of Finland in chaps and a vest. I'm not sure where he's come from or where he's going. He pulls a soft pack of cigarettes from a hidden pocket, then heads up the hill to the magnificent view.

CHAPTER THREE

AN ILLUSTRATED DICTIONARY OF ornithologists' swear words. A pattern book for digital fabric design. The story of a winsome loner who finds mystical doors to travel through the universe. It's a busy morning. I need to focus. Except I'm distracted by the bits and pieces I've come know about Darrel.

Firsthand, for myself, one thing I know about him: he's been working on an art project, whittling or carving for several weeks now. He doesn't make much noise. But sawdust has been raining down through the floorboards, his shavings sprinkling between my exposed beams.

"It's not a big deal." I tried to minimize it with Kenny. He'd caught a glimpse when I was meeting my morning delivery, pushing me aside, pressing through the doorway, full-on ashamed of the mess. When he looked up, he was shocked by the porous divide between us.

"You've ripped out your ceiling. The drywall or whatever." He stood in my place and studied the exposed joists and wiring. "Not much privacy. Anything else coming through?"

"No, no," I told him. "Not to worry. Just some sawdust."

"It's very cool though," he told me, toeing some dust. "What Darrel's working on—it's a masthead. A big one. The kind of thing they used to put on the front of a ship. The prow."

He told me to wait, then he dashed up the steps and back down again with some sketches in hand.

"Very cool," he said again, folding it out for me. Darrel's drawings showed schematics for a big, curvy woman, all busty and streamlined, like you'd see on the front of an old pirate ship. But with a masculine chin, square and stubbled, striving over a pair of ample boobs. The chin alone would generate a lot of dust without even including shavings from the bosom.

I held one of the sketches up to the window, eyeing it up there, suspended in the sky. "We've gotta put it up."

Kenny looked at me, a big grin spreading. "Yes!" he said and stomped where he stood, a little sawdust rising up around his shoes. "I was really dreading coming down here and talking through this."

But it was just what we need here. Something crazy and beautiful to counterbalance the freshly tidied corners across the street. It would blend well regardless, unnoticed unless you looked for it, like an oversized weather vane or a filigreed lightning rod or gargoyles sitting quietly on a high cathedral roof. I held the sketch up, and I was confident it belonged there, above our column of rounded windows. I was also happy to see Kenny so happy. His grin made me grin. And as a bonus, it might cut down on people peering into my space.

But the sawdust has stopped. I haven't seen Darrel in days, not since the ambulance. The next time I spot Kenny, we're in the library basement, nodding to each other across a stuffy room. This time the presentation is led by a small group, red-eyed city planners and overdressed developers informing us about the new transit hub down the hill. The room is packed—the shoving seniors are there, along with several others, making up a contingent near the cookie buffet—and a lot of new faces are crammed in as well. It's early evening, an after-work hour, and from the looks on most faces, it feels like it's already dragged on too long.

The comment period is testy. I'd thought people were bored, but it turns out they were pissed, waiting their turn to register their revulsion. No one wants the new hub, no one likes the design, and no one seems to know the elected representatives in the room. It is universal, and it is broad, and it is something to watch generations come together and rally their disgust. The new service and amenity is totally unwelcome. It's also signed for and paid for and will break ground soon.

I navigate toward Kenny and ask about Darrel in a whisper. He tells me he's fine. "But still in the hospital. He's still got a ways to go."

He points to the big visual aids on easels and in a more careful whisper says he's on the fence. He says he's worried about noise first, then the bump in traffic. "But I think it might actually boost property values."

I nod along, trying to catch up with his thinking. "I love a lot of things in theory. But you can't really know…"

He looks at me quickly and lowers his voice again. "You should know Darrel and I are working on things. He's started new meds, and they've complicated things."

I nod again and, somehow, want to acknowledge what's between us—how too much is between us. I think we've shared more than average neighbors do. More than I'm used to, more than I think is normal, plus the intensity of his sharing continues, despite the close crowd and the fevered pitch of the room.

A line of people passes between us, pushing their way out of the basement. No one likes the developers' responses, and no one wants to hear more. The easels and the visual aids are getting a good jostle.

I also see the old woman in thick glasses coming straight for me, the one from the bludgeoning talk on poverty. Her gentleman ally, the one who's quick to shove, follows close behind. I have to step back to the stairs and the exit, and Kenny feels the same need to move.

"I need to get home," he pleads with me, taking me by the arm, leading me toward the stairs, and doing his best to bury us in the crowd trudging up. The agitation is thick. People are grumbling, stranger to stranger, sharing their frustration in the crowded stair-well—*Did you see those drawings? Is there no way to stop this? How did this ever get past the planning stages?* Pressed close as we are, Kenny uses the climb to share more about Darrel, whispering something about his insurance. "It's weirdly not easy. He's had some legal issues."

"Of course," I say, looking over my shoulder. I'm pretty sure we've ditched them, the aggressive old people. I think I've avoided another dustup. Once we're on the main floor and the congestion starts to clear, backpacks and cell phones come out of nowhere, and the meeting gets recapped at brand-new decibels.

I wasn't sure what I'd say or how I'd react. I'd prefer to forget the whole thing. I still don't know what that old woman thinks she knows about me, and I don't feel like finding out in this crowd. But I'm happy to stop on the library's front steps, in the middle of neighbors, a crowd I don't typically experience this way. These are the people I usually watch out my windows, walking downhill for their morning commute and up again on their way back home. They look at me now like I'm vaguely familiar, like they can't quite decide if they know me or not.

"Hello, hello," I greet them as they pass me. "Have a good evening. Enjoy your night." I'm a little baffled by how different they look from this close, in this light. A man I'd thought was a grandfather is way too young, with facial hair and a fedora I couldn't see past before. A second wave brings more commotion, a circus of parents and children unloading from the after-work storytime upstairs. They also hurry past me, rushing down the front steps.

The kids I don't recognize; they move too quickly, and most days, I think, they're in transit before I sit down at my desk. They push past me like I'm nobody, a stranger in their way. This close to them, it feels very weird, very off, not knowing their names.

Kenny is looking at me, still not sure what the problem is, but sure as ever he needs to get home. He reaches over the kids, pulls me to the curbside, and finally, it's time to go: the seniors are emerging, looking over the little heads, trying to see where I ran off to.

"Can we pick up the pace?" Kenny grabs at my sleeve. He says that like he's not interested in my answer, and he doesn't mind silence that follows, either. He's more focused on navigating the next couple blocks. Still gripping my sleeve, he pushes us past strollers, guides us over leashes, and cuts us through the line outside a coffee shop. The transit hub is old business by now. There's nothing to discuss there. The only priority is getting home fast.

I see now how Kenny operates, at one speed only, in one direction exclusively, on a path of his own forging, no matter what. It's the same intensity as when he talked about Darrel. Everyone is a bystander, a nonaligned spectator, outsiders who don't serve his most immediate goal. Ahead, a pair of buskers on amplified washboards are playing outside an overflowing restaurant, but he pulls me even closer, avoiding the nuisance. His curiosity is focused. That's the kindest way to put it.

I feel like we left the hub unresolved, like we really should be talking about the overwhelming hate for it. It's really not so simple, a complex issue we can't run away from. On paper, it's a blue-sky, big-tent project, but in practice, on those posters tonight, it's a horrible thing. It promises both the best and the worst of progressive thinking. A mixed-use transit-rich market-diverse project that feels doomed to a whole lot of dank scenarios. The developers' plans include three and four floors of residential units over a line of plug-and-play retail services. All of that is needed. Every laundry and barber and burrito outpost is overcrowded in this town. Every commercial corridor feels like it's carrying a thousand or so extra pairs of feet. The hub development will stretch two city blocks, rising above a new subway station. The subway stop is the one bright spot, a rare and glamorous bit of infrastructure. As is, the corners are crammed day and night, locals and outsiders switching lines and directions. Just down the hill, a block or so away, it's a messy crash of day laborers and stock traders, drug dealers and tech execs, drag queens and quinceañeras, late-model Teslas and old-model Hondas and accordion buses that huff and puff through their own pneumatic lanes. With the hub, all that business and all those characters will go underground, creating better flow, better comity, even as the station, its amenities and its new residents—four hundred souls—will boost, exponentially, the neighborhood's use and traffic.

The initial renderings are sketchy. What was unveiled tonight in the library basement was indelibly inelegant. Too rough to avoid doubt and suspicion. It is too big, too monolithic, and too slab-like—a future wasteland of ill-defined franchises, where overhead, overworked parents are expected to raise kids and grow old. It all comes too late for my evicted neighbors. I wonder if the dealer kid would've found clients down there.

"Did you hear the response?" I ask Kenny under my breath. When the renderings went up, a lot of the crowd gasped—the ugliness was just so overwhelming, plus the scale of the monstrosity, the lack of variance, the missed windows, and the total void of charm. "There is nothing enchanting about the hub, Kenny." As if that were unreasonable, asking too much from a basic public space. "For a local bus stop with a few trains running through it, shouldn't charm and beauty be basic requirements?"

"*Charm?*" Kenny says. "You want a bus stop that's *charming?*"

I stop myself. "You're right. Of course. Bigger things to take care of."

But it's happening anyway, it's coming regardless of the reaction or the gasping or the turnout in the library basement. Existing businesses are closing, old structures are coming down, the subway will get extended soon, and several acres of concrete will bloom and blossom, like white mold on an old treasure map. Funding is secured. Permits have been rushed. What's zoned and rezoned will soon be as one. The meeting tonight was just a formality, despite the outrage.

I watched the politicos rub their foreheads as their constituents elbowed their charts and easels. If we didn't know their names before, we'll know them from now on. The developers, on the other hand, seemed totally unruffled. Four reps from banks and real estate groups stood girded and ready, arms crossed with stiff smiles under the library's fluorescents.

"There's no nice way to say it: it's the influx," Kenny tells me, serious as ever. "It's safe here now. It just got safe, really. Look at all the women who moved in across the street." Kenny is the one looking over his shoulder now, lowering his voice again. "I'm talking about people who come and go for no reason. That subway will connect us to a lot of new populations. Board a train thirty miles from here and, just like that, step onto our front steps. Easy access from every corner of the world."

"Kenny…" I feel like I should scold him. It's not a popular position, excluding anyone, and I'm not sure his take is very enlightened. He's been here for years, and the intersection down the hill has been crazy since forever—since long before his arrival. The new hub will only bring more of what we live with, the mix that makes our hill special, a steep climb away from the everyday hustle.

He still grips my sleeve, still leading the way slightly, and even though we've cleared the restaurants and the crowds at the cafés, he's not slowing down. A young couple walks toward us. They address as if we're together—"Lovely evening, boys"—just like any couple on a notably brisk stroll.

"See," Kenny says, and I get his point. We are a tolerant tribe here, or a well-oiled machine, or a shifting menagerie that somehow coexists. We have very live-and-let-live expectations. To get to and from work and to get along in the in-between, we don't require many agreements or even a lot of cooperation. For the most part, we get along in library basements. I can't remember the last time we looked for a local consensus, until this hub popped up—with across-the-board disapproval—and it turns out, we've screwed that up. We responded too late. No one opposed it previously. Nobody showed up until nothing could be changed.

"I take too much for granted," I tell Kenny now. I take it for granted that Kenny feels safe here, that the women feel safe here, that my window on the world is always calm and beautiful.

We keep quiet for the rest of the walk, and not another word about Darrel. A loud noise not so far away—fireworks or some sort of celebratory explosion—makes us pick up the pace. At least we assume it's celebratory. Once home, out my window, the skyline sparkles on my way to bed.

In the morning, at my desk, there are cheery prospects. Good news on a book we published earlier this year, a small one about the spleen and its role in medicine, literature, and pop culture—but in a fun way, it's funny, an encyclopedic knowledge delivered with a light touch. It's showed up on three best-of lists this week.

Our editor in St. Louis has sent a note with the news, asking if I've seen the lists and, maybe, heard rumors about a major award somewhere in the works. I don't write back right away, distracted by his sign-off. *St. Louis*, it says. Same as always. Same as every day. I don't think about it much, but I have a connection, the city means something to me: as a child, I was in the big shiny arch when it was struck during an electrical storm.

The arch shook violently, then vibrated quietly. I remember the people, the strangers around me, reaching for the walls to steady themselves. Strikes can't be uncommon. It's a big bent lightning rod on the edge of a river. Right away, a long line formed for the elevators, wonders of the modern age, somehow rigged to go both sideways and up, like something out of Wonka. I was told I was safe. There was no need to panic. I was welcome to stay and watch the storm pass. I was alone there, separated from my chaperones and the group I was touring with. "Son," I heard, as a heavy, hairy hand landed on my shoulder, "you're welcome to stay just as long as you want."

It was creepy. And scary. Even more than the lightning bolt. I followed the hand up and saw a man of exaggerated height, bald and so tall he had to hunch against the curved ceiling. He looked as if he was coming down at me—while the arch still buzzed and others were still scrambling, including my guardian making a beeline for the exit.

I was in St. Louis for a dance competition, as a child competitor in the youth category. It's a lost talent I try to avoid bringing up. There are pictures somewhere of my boy-body in tights, at the barre, at rehearsal, arms elevated just so in the third or fifth position, looking earnest and strained and for all the world like this could never be mocked. Like those professionally arranged photos could never resurface and I could never be embarrassed by my middle-school self. I have no idea where the confidence to parade around in boy-tights has gone. But the competition was intense, and without going too deep or digging up those old pictures, I know what I learned from St. Louis: the value of commitment and seriousness.

I was plenty nimble to escape the arch's giant—a stranger whose intentions I never learned till much later—but the city also spurred some of my earliest soul-searching. When I got home, I scoured our library's children's section and stumbled on an illustrated history— Russian versus French versus Viennese ballets, and the corrupt aristocracies that bankrolled and shaped them. Then I found the same influence on music and painting. And then on buildings and cities.

Behind them all, popes and duchies and industrialists. Something sinister had always decided what's beautiful. That was the clear lesson from St. Louis. I didn't quit straightaway, but over the next several months, I backed off from dancing, I put my energy into reading, and I committed to one day producing beautiful things free from ambiguous threats or hidden influence.

"I've got nothing," I write to St. Louis this morning. "Nothing about longlists or shortlists or award buzz or anything. I haven't even seen a big review lately."

I have to focus this morning. I have to zero in on the spleen, its impact on the world, a magical history in less than two hundred pages. Crisp, deft, original, and revelatory. It belongs on a winners' shelf. It deserves a gold sticker. I'm delighted that others are thinking the same way.

"Keep an ear to the ground," St. Louis writes back. "We could use a win. A little pick-me-up would do us good."

I'm not sure what that means. I could read too much into it. The puppy calendars are doing well, so our accounts are in order. The book on the spleen is selling as expected. Otherwise, we're having a fairly typical year: a semi-fictional biography of a lesser-known Borgia, an anthology of essays by first-year gynecologists, a novel about warring families in an uber-bro future. Poems by dogs for dogs. A manifesto redefining refrigeration. It's a fickle business, getting people's attention. I never know where some books will land, but this year, like most, so far, so good.

In my queue of messages, I see a post from a very disgruntled author. At a prestigious journal, she's fictionalized a conversation I thought was private, a hatchet job she titled "How to Teach Your Editor to Think."

She was enraged by my response to her unconventional use of capital letters. I enjoyed them, actually, but she interpreted my enthusiasm as sophomoric and patronizing. My skin prickles. It feels like an intrusion, and with her spiced-up story, everyone will look at me like a fraud and a fool. A world of whispers and nothing to be done about it. Never room in this business for dimensional doubt.

At the curb below, a dog walker struggles to rein in her clients, bulldogs, pugs, and shorthairs pulling hard on a rainbow of leashes, yelping at her, snapping at each other, twisting their leads until there's no moving on. She digs into her fanny pack, passes out lumpy treats, and more furry chaos follows, while the barking intensifies. The walker howls back, laughing along with them. Then she happens to look up. Five snouts look up, too, and a lot of tails are wagging. Not everything is rotten everywhere.

CHAPTER FOUR

THE LIBRARY BASEMENT IS a musty space with old polished paneling and round porthole windows up high near the ceiling. Big wooden reading tables are often pushed to the side, put into service under coffee urns and platters of treats. A few years ago, after the city reopened a score of shuttered libraries, concerned locals funded a spit-and-polish campaign that revivified the basement and brought arts-and-crafts fixtures back to the reading room upstairs. The whole thing is surprising to first-time visitors, a throwback to former glories. It probably wasn't the best setting for the hub unveiling.

The turnout was standing room only, and the lemon bars were cleared before things even started. Local council folk introduced the reps from the developer, a man in a slim suit and three women in pencil skirts, each taking their turn in button-down talks. One woman addressed "our pain points," then the man talked us through how other cities have addressed similar problems, and finally a second woman lifted the sheets on the big posters, revealing the hub's basic design. Gasps followed. "No, no, no."

The old woman was particularly vocal, and as Kenny pulled me up the stairs, before we started rushing home, I noticed two women from the building across the street. They were standing in the back, mostly typing on their phones. They were a unified pair, the only ones nodding, with four thumbs up as the sheets fell and the designs were revealed. They started applauding, which prompted a few others, but only a very few. They talked sort of loudly between themselves, distilling the presentation into a simple argument: with more people, we'll have more services, and more convenience and safety, all leading to the quick remaking of their new neighborhood. A solid move with benefits for everyone, which they were eager to welcome a block or so down the hill from their front stoop.

"We're pro-progress," Marleen told me as she put on her jacket. I'd just made it up the stairs to the library's front steps, the first wave was still passing me. I noticed her and nodded. She paused and nodded like she knew me—I had waved hello from my window on her moving day, but I could tell that didn't stick. Now all she wanted was some distance from the library: she clearly saw her support was out of step. As the crowd passed us now, most turned around to check her out, one of the oddballs who was clapping. Folks closest to us noticed and took a step or two back. With space cleared around us, she looked at me earnestly, trying to keep me focused on her, even as her partner caught up, touched her arm, and walked ahead through the crowd to the curb.

Marleen's T-shirt made a statement about her Chinese-American heritage, not the kind of thing I feel comfortable repeating. I learned later that she works as a private chef and globetrots a lot for her CEO client, always on call and at his heels, seeing the world from the twin views of penthouse kitchens and local markets. Fascinating. Truly. She looked like she'd be comfortable in any setting. Like she'd be herself anywhere. Intense, not so smiley, and always probing.

She stood there and didn't look away, waiting for more me to say more, until Max, her partner, started badgering from the curb, phone in hand. "We gotta bolt," she said, waving Marleen over. "This thing was the bust, and the car is almost here."

Max didn't recognize me either. Max is tall and solid and seems not to stand fully straight because of it, probably to accommodate everyone around her. I also learned later that she works in venture capital, after Berkeley, then Stanford. A native, a local, and their apartment is always dark. Neither one spends much time there, as far as I can tell. So I'm not sure how they made it to the presentation, why they're spending time in a library basement, and how they can argue the hub is good.

Maybe professional connections. Like the hub's developer is a client of Max's or the architect is a friend of one or the other, or they've crossed paths with someone in local government who claims to have an honest stake in all of this.

"I just worry about the traffic and bringing more people to the neighborhood." In a nutshell, that's how my best defense came out. No one asked me. Neither Max nor Marleen had inquired about my opinion. But Marleen seemed to want one. She hadn't looked away yet.

But then Max zeroed in. I saw her turn from the curb, push her way toward me, and make a very sour face, like she couldn't leave what I said well enough alone. Once we stood nose to nose there, something else arrived with her, a particularly bad attitude, like I wasn't appreciating her time and attention, the effort she'd made to be there that evening, and the extra effort she was putting in now, doubling back to focus on me. "Everything you've thought of has been taken care of," she told me. "It's all mitigated. In the design. It's all taken care of." Then she squeezed me on the shoulder and softened her tone a little. "Oh, honey," she said before she turned and walked away again, this time pulling Marleen along with her.

Then Kenny grabbed my arm again, and we picked up our pace past the restaurants and cafés. Before we got too far, I saw Marleen and Max duck into a car, one that was waiting for them, the driver rushing to the curb and opening the door for them, in a weirdly sinister way. Not a regular on-demand car. More like an old-school black sedan with a committed man at their service.

"Do you know Max or any of the others across the street?" I asked Kenny. The windows on their car were tinted, so I couldn't point to them as they sped past.

He shook his head, and before we got home, we heard the small explosion. Like a firework or a cherry bomb, something big enough to make us feel it in the bones in our head. Maybe we were silly to think it was celebratory. Kenny and I looked at each other, then pretty much jogged the rest of the way, to make sure our building was still intact. No fire, no alarms, nothing imminent or frightening. Except for a generous puff of smoke rising over the women's building across the street.

Max and Marleen were nowhere in sight, and the windows of their apartment were still dark. Whatever it was—if not a quick batch of fireworks, then maybe a small gas leak or an odd cooking mishap—their building was undisturbed, too. No one came rushing out, and in the next hour or so, from my window, no police or fire trucks pulled up.

It was almost as if the small explosions weren't happening. Or an explosion could be small enough to not worry about. No fires, no damage, so nothing to do. Nothing risky afoot until the sirens start coming. The biggest commotion this morning comes over the wires. Award buzz for the spleen book is continuing to build, and the hubbub is spurring new proposals and manuscripts. A big rainbow of stories, a bubbling hot pot of ideas coming our way, fueled only by the whiff of a win. But in the mix—and I'm lucky to spot it—there's a request that requires—demands—an immediate response.

Beau Bram, the novelist, the bestselling novelist, the award-winning, widely acclaimed super-selling novelist, the one who sells

and sells and sells—he has a project he'd like to do with us. I pause
long and hard. The note is from him personally, not an agent or an
intermediary. Which adds to its oddness, because we've never met,
we have no connection, and I have no idea why he'd reach out to us.

"Why us?" I ask St. Louis. "What's going on here? Have you
been chumming up to Beau Bram lately?"

"Not at all," he tells me. "I've already checked with the others,
too. No contact. No connections."

"It doesn't make sense." Why go small with us when he's already
in the big time? Why work on the margins when he can lead the
pack? Why would he guarantee himself lower sales and less income?
Why take the extra risk? And why start all over, getting to know a
new publisher, a new editor, a new publicity process?

"My first thought: *it sucks*." The book probably stinks. It's probably a project his regular editor rejected so he's sending it down to us.
Throwing us a bone. His sloppy seconds. Leftovers wrapped in his
major brand name. I wait for St. Louis's thoughts on that.

"Only one way to find out!" His response is almost chirping.

It must be a minor work and a favor he thinks he's doing us—but
here's the tricky part. Whatever it is, we'll have to be grateful. We'll
have to respond graciously and strategically to his query.

"Think about it," I reply to St. Louis. "To reject it will cause fric-
tion on levels I don't even know about. You don't say no easily to an
offer like this. It's one of those gambits that can go either way."

Which quickly leads to my second thought: *We can't afford it*.
The price tag has to be steep. You don't give away something this
rich…There's gotta be a hitch. Or it's just a mistake, a misunder-
standing, presuming we can afford to pay what he gets from a massive publisher with international reach.

I hover on the Saved queue, but then download it straightaway.
Thankfully, it's short, a shortish novel, and as I begin reading, it's rich

and poignant and eerily, magically geared toward me. Outside on my corner, there's a man in a tutu with an accordion juggling beach balls, but I ignore him to focus on Bram's manuscript.

The story follows two gay men who happen to be a lot like Darrel and Kenny. Right off the bat, I stop and do a search: *Is Beau Bram gay?* I find photos of a middle-aged white man, bearded, salt and peppered, looking either deeply serious or grinning uninhibited, where his eyes disappear except for a nice spark. He looks like an accomplished writer. His photos have that intention. His listed status is single with no divorce and no kids, which might just mean he's devoted to his work. I turn back to his manuscript, and I'm already distracted, wondering if this book is his way of coming out. Is that a goldmine or a quagmire? Do I really want to get into that? Wouldn't more dog calendars be a better, safer bet?

His protagonists are Danny and Christian, two affluent swells shacking up in present-day London. The initial conflict is with a Muslim shopkeeper who treats them rudely enough to be a running joke but then crosses a line when he kicks Danny out. It's late on the weekend, they'd been to a concert, and they'd had too much to drink. Danny makes a joke of his own, reaching over the counter for the storekeeper's open collar and the chain around his neck. The response is explosive and escalates into violence. Danny ends up with a bloodied nose and black eye, bad enough to send him to the hospital.

I am fifty pages in when I feel like I should stop. I don't want to, I'm seduced, on the edge of my seat and scrolling fast. "It's good. It's not junk," I report to St. Louis. But it's also late, and I'm not following so closely, missing nuances and connections I should savor and catalogue. I close the computer and go to bed just when, in the novel, Christian is pounding on his neighbor's door, asking for help with an ambulance.

I'm just sitting with the parallels, not making too much of them, letting the overlaps stand and the concurrences just be. It's a different story already, set in multicultural London and dealing with a different set of societal gaps. It's ridiculous to look for meaning in coincidences, and in the morning, the correlations might not be so obvious. Neighbors knock on neighbors' doors all the time, everywhere.

And then I hear Kenny pounding down the stairs, then pounding on my door, then yelling for me to come out. I'm already tucked in, but I suddenly feel like I'm in a Beau Bram novel, like the city is aswirl and I'm about to be caught up in an exceptionally profound series of events.

I jump up and meet Kenny in the vestibule.

"Another explosion," he tells me, wrapped in a blanket, a plaid onesie underneath.

I'm wrapped in a blanket, too, pajama bottoms pulled high. But I've missed the explosion. I didn't hear anything, and there's nothing else out here except empty streets. We look at each other, both uncomfortable with our blankets.

"Did you hear it?" he asks, a little deflated, pointing into the night.

The women's building is still dark. But when I look again, I can see a plume of smoke, a smudge of gray-black against the blue-black sky, rising above the backside of the building. Again, no one is responding. The building is undisturbed. No one congregates on the sidewalk. No one else seems to notice or show concern. No authorities or rescue vehicles are racing to get here.

"Maybe it's a science project. Maybe someone's just tinkering." I'm already yawning, and I look to Kenny.

"Maybe," he says.

This would be the second explosion across the street, and as a mystery, it's uncomfortable and not so easy to let go of—because it's not a live-and-let-live happening. Because these explosions, however minor they might be, could endanger us all, sparking a fire that might ignite the entire hill. New and old construction sit nose to nose here, squeezed in tight and close. A tinderbox. A kindling pile. I've watched the heavy blue tarps flap in the wind, temporary covers stretched over burnt rooflines, struggling to protect what's left. They've been sitting on two for over a year now. Three more have been added in the past couple days, covering the remains from the most recent fires. They're all dotting the slope, so taut and blue.

"Thank you for waking me." I pull my blanket tighter. Kenny does the same. We agree to do our best to stay on alert. At least the skyline from our vestibule is beautiful and twinkly.

"Glamorous," Kenny says.

"All night long," I say.

In the morning, there's no change. No visible blast marks, no missing windows. Not even an open gate. Calm prevails. Order is sanctified. It's early on a Saturday, so there's even less traffic than usual, limited to a few joggers and a solitary father pushing another pricey stroller at an ungentle pace.

"This is why we need books," I write to St. Louis. "To light bigger fires and really amplify things."

He responds immediately. "Don't know what you're talking about. Need to focus on Bram and his manuscript this morning."

In the next fifty pages, Beau Bram's story keeps unfolding, with the messy wonderland of London as a marvelous backdrop. I pick up with Christian pounding on his neighbor's door. Covered in sweat. Middle of the night. I know what I'm expecting. But here, in Bram's story, his neighbor doesn't respond. He doesn't get up and answer Christian's yelling.

I would never do that. What kind of person would? What sort of neighbor doesn't respond to desperate calls in the middle of the night? Again, I'm too distracted to keep reading, sidetracked by doubts.

I would never have considered ignoring Kenny, pulling up the blankets and staying in bed. It's a small but critical detail, and it puts me off enough to stop. In a single passage, Bram's London is not so marvelous. It feels artificial. Kind of forced and faked. I'm disappointed, and the parallels with my world start to feel annoying.

Bram is also straying from his usual formula: quiet domestic stories with troubling underbellies that suddenly turn on an unexpected dime, twisting on a perfect gesture that leaves whole households, whole communities, and in subtext, most of civilization on the brink.

His books feel as if they're lifted from the nineteenth century and as if Mr. Bram spent time there himself. In his first, a La Jolla stable boy–orphan discovers his massive overlooked inheritance and spends the next thirty years and three hundred pages in mesmerizing avoidance of ponies and races. He makes himself into the ideal husband, father, and community pillar, until one triggering word from a drunk retiring jockey makes his enchanted universe fall apart. Social circles turn against him, business partners leave him hanging, and his children begin drifting to faraway coasts. Or not. He's not sure. It could be his imagination, just a made-up pattern, something he's seeing since his head's been blown up, spun round by a word with unknown power, as if a spurned hypnotist-magician has returned to take everything an orphan thought he deserved. That word was "artichoke," and for critics, it's common code for a deeply constructed turning point, as in "nobody bites an artichoke like Beau Bram at a jockey club." In Bram's most recent novel, his thirteenth, a young immigrant girl lands a windfall from distant relatives and suffers the same sort of spellbinding delusion, also for three hundred pages or so.

But this latest is a thriller and a far stretch from his regular award-winning brilliance. I told St. Louis it wasn't junk, and I look forward to his opinion, but I'm ready to chuck it now. Bram's story isn't landing right. That's not the way neighbors anywhere should treat other. And even though I know they do—people ignore others' troubles all the time, every day, in every walk of life—I feel out of sync with Beau Bram. The neighbor's negligence, his disregard—it's so casual, so minor, it feels dismissive and deeply wrong.

In the pages that follow, Danny gets kidnapped, Christian is convinced the shopkeeper is to blame, and London explodes with a story of revenge, social phobia, and unbridled outrage. Gripping stuff— which I read a little slower, through a different lens now, tripped up with questions about the author.

When I look up, on the sidewalk, a young man and woman are holding hands, watching me read. Now that I've stopped, the show seems to be over. They look away, turn together, and head up the street.

CHAPTER FIVE

ONE WEEK WAS ONLY slipstream. Another brought a string of academics in heat, long-winded episodes set in garret bedrooms and Quonset-hut married-student housing. St. Louis and I, we are quiet about what we're looking for; we don't specialize, and we don't always rely on pedigree. Which makes it hard for submitters, who don't know which chord to strike. Personally, I keep a low profile, so I'm not cornered at parties or hounded at events. I've also never admitted that I'm not really sure what the heck slipstream is about.

St. Louis reads too and has a say on the final list. I am no genius of trends. I'm not a prodigious guru. But I keep my nose pointed in several directions, to have a sense of what's coming, what people will read next, and now and then, we miss the mark altogether. Sometimes trends don't move like anyone expected. Sometimes things shift to unplotted places. Hurricanes. Elections. Threats from overseas. Unforeseen events can shape expectations and turn readers' appetites in surprising ways. At a certain point, you can say how things will go, and also that things will probably be blown off course.

I'm preoccupied by last night's explosion. There's still no evidence this morning, no sign that it ever happened, and I try not to stare across the street. It's a mystery, especially given the neighborhood's new direction. With or without the transit hub plan, I thought we'd moved on from our sketchy past.

There's some noise out front, someone moving in the vestibule. I check the clock and the street and get that it's the delivery. Lennon from EggSprout, the daily service that keeps me stocked—milk, coffee, juices, greens, but mostly prepared meals that only need heating up. It is a turnkey operation that fundamentally sustains me, that keeps me focused, that allows me to stick to my desk throughout the day. Things cost a little extra, sometimes a lot extra, but I rationalize it with the convenience and the extra screen time.

I usually let Lennon come and go without bothering him. He's on a tight schedule. He doesn't need me to slow him. Daily, he runs to and from a black EggSprout van double-parked on the corner.

But I catch him this morning. For once, he's sitting on the front steps, legs spread below him, taking a minute to blow smoke from a joint.

He offers it to me. I decline, like I always do, and I ask what he's heard about the local explosions. "Any talk on the street? Any idea what's going on?"

"Drug lab?" he says, scrunching up his face. He's an oversized guy with a full, bushy beard and a mop-head he's stuffed under a black Giants cap. His thick legs stretch across four steps. "Could be. You don't think so?"

He can see my skepticism. "Too upscale," I tell him and nod at the women's building. "People who can afford places like that don't usually go in for manufacturing."

"Got it," he tells me. "Then I couldn't really say."

"Nobody's said anything? And you haven't heard them?"

He gets to his feet, not looking at me but clear now that my stairs are not a chill space. "I should get going," he says. "I don't talk to anybody, and you're just about the only one who orders around here."

He's down at the sidewalk before I can say more. "Shocking," I tell him.

"Not really," he shouts back, giving a wave while he jogs to the van. I take in the stack of supplies he left and close the door without locking it, this morning's small act of faith.

When Sylvie and I first moved in, some hooligans poured glue in our garage lock. It was pointless prank-vandalism on a late October night. Irritating, a hassle, and I didn't think too much of it. We weren't obvious targets. Who would vandalize us? Why would we deserve that? I doubted it was meant specifically for us, but Sylvie was convinced it was the dealer kid across the street, trying to be threatening, marking his territory when we first showed up.

"It's so old school," I argued. "So small scale. It's hard to imagine it's *supposed* to be threatening. I think someone did it as a goof, just because it was there. A totally random choice to glue our garage shut. Kids out on a bender just screwing with things."

"But the kid across the street..." Sylvie was serious. "There's something off about him. His blinds are always pulled, but I've heard him up there. He yells at me a lot."

"What do you mean he yells at you?" That was the first I'd heard of it.

"Catcalls. Rude sounds. Vulgar, nasty stuff."

"Vulgar? Since when?"

"Since forever. Since we moved in."

I gave her a look. I couldn't believe she hadn't told me.

My reaction perturbed her. She interpreted it as a scolding, as if she should have come running or needed my protection. As if I were somehow specially equipped. "He's a creep. A perv type. I've seen him do it to other women, too."

"So he's marking his space with the glue in our locks?"

She shrugged like it was obvious. "Sure," she tells me. "You know," she goes on, "it's remarkable how oblivious you walk around here."

And with that, a common chorus. Obliviousness, blind spots, insensitivities. My general lack of mindfulness. The list began to grow. Sylvie and I did not see our neighborhood the same way. We experienced our lives here with fundamental differences. Crossing the street to avoid an alley, crossing it again to skip the bus stop, avoiding a corner store because of its night clerks, and generally staying out of a notorious bottle shop—that was just her short list, the trouble spots she navigated. The list was constantly being added to, the local geography of dangers, where she did and did not feel safe.

"It's just common sense," she told me, and I watched her anger escalate. "It's not like I'm trembling whenever I leave the house."

"Christ," I told her. "Why haven't you told me this? If things are that bad, why the hell do we live here?"

"Because it's not just here…" She scoffed and shook her head.

End of conversation. Start of something big.

The list lived on as a source of tension, and I could tell she was lengthening it in deliberate ways. She wasn't looking for danger. But she enjoyed reminding me of it, routinely and regularly.

I couldn't admit it to her, but it's why I moved my desk to the window. In part, so I could keep an eye out, watch her come and go and to see what she experienced and what the hell I could do to maybe intercede. Her criticism hurt, but I was genuinely worried. Maybe I could sharpen my skills. Become usefully mindful. Finally witness the vulgar, nasty world she walked through every day.

Once my desk was there, visible from other windows, the kid across the street stopped his yelling and badgering. I don't know if I should take credit, but something good came from it. The first time I caught him, I stood up, crossed my arms, and just plain stared. Let him known he was seen. After that I only saw him pacing the corner, fingering the stash in his black cargo pants.

"So brave," Sylvie told me and patted me on the head.

I didn't know what else to do. I could watch, I could ask, I could listen, all of that. I cleaned the glue from the locks, and I kept an eye on our sidewalk. But I think what she really wanted was confrontation. Frontline action. Something that would put me face to face and in her boots.

"It's not just me," she told me, very near the end. She was holding a coffee, about to head out the door. It had been a silent morning. We hadn't spoken since the night before. We got showered and dressed, downed a little breakfast, all of it without sharing a word. But she had something to say before she left for work. "Maggie had it even worse with that kid."

Maggie had lived down the block and had been an executive at a furniture retailer, before she and her husband moved two doors down to raise their first child. They'd left an expensive high rise as soon as she got pregnant, coming here for a more residential vibe. The mix of neighbors was part of the draw, an organic amalgam, the kind of blend you can't buy at private play groups.

"Maggie?" I said. "I didn't know she got hassled." I was already at my desk settling in, scanning my queue, at least pretending to work until Sylvie left.

"She heard from him every day. Every time she went by with little Agnes and the stroller. Ugly, weird, sexual stuff."

I was genuinely baffled. "Who assaults a mom with a kid?" I couldn't believe no one had told me this. "What kind of thrill could he get out of that?"

"He just needs to be violent," Sylvie said, rushing to get out. "I don't think it's more specific than that."

She closed the door. My stomach churned, and I watched her join the stream of office workers headed down the hill for the jammed intersection. Neither Sylvie nor Maggie were edgy dressers.

They didn't walk around trying to shock or titillate. Sylvie, especially, was sophisticated and understated, and whenever I'd seen Maggie, she looked remarkably composed, like she was still at the office instead of at home with her first child all day.

"For the record," I told Sylvie that night, "I've never thought it was *just you*. I don't know why you said that this morning. I'm just trying to understand what's been going on."

Sylvie gave me another shrug. I felt put in my place, and like I'd never catch up.

That night, the scolding continued. "Maggie warned me before they moved away. She tried lots of things, yelling back, ringing doorbells, talking to his neighbors in the building. She called the cops a couple times, but they never came. Several times she tried to engage him from the sidewalk, talking up at him. 'What's your deal?' 'Do you need something?' Things like that, as calm as she could."

"What did he do?" I had to ask. "How did the kid react?"

But Sylvie was already looking down at her phone. She was done with our conversation. "He was a creep. He stayed behind his creepy blinds. Made more creepy noises."

I watched her take off her shoes and head for the bedroom. "Blech," I offered.

"Right," she said, not really looking up. "Blech."

Maggie's quick move to Berkeley made more sense now. I'd heard two rationales: access to better schools and a strong seller's market. With the sale of their house, they'd make a ton of money, enough to cover tuition bills if they acted fast. But the kid across the street was another reason to go.

"How does a boy turn out like that?" Sylvie said before she closed the bedroom door. She moved behind it before I could think what to say.

Now and then, I still saw his filthy blinds rustle, but with no particular pattern, at no particular time. Day or night, really. His presence or his threat couldn't be counted on. He never shouted at me, and it felt even more creepy because of that.

What was he up to? No school, no work? Why didn't he have better things to do all day? That was my big question, especially on busy days, at my desk across from him, my new sentinel position. Why wasn't someone scolding him into shape?

But since then, and very recently, specifically since getting shoved in the library basement, I've got a new perspective: do people on the street see me the same way? The angry seniors probably heard about trouble on this corner and then spotted me sitting up here all day. That would justify everything, their disgust, their public shaming. If they mistook me for him, I don't blame them for that. And now that I've been through it, getting shoved by neighbors, I have to agree with Sylvie. I'm disappointed I never did it, never went down, crossed the street, and gave the weird kid a good poke in the chest.

After she left, Sylvie ended up with a rich tech founder. An age-appropriate man who'd been a schoolteacher but turned some textbooks into an industry platform. A lucrative act of imagination, an inspired idea for which he's been rewarded. From photos I've found, he is tall and athletic, dashing and serious, the kind of partner you'd want good friends to end up with. He is also one of the city's new invisible hands, a guiding spirit that moves through the fog and hills now.

Sylvie is part of it, intimately tied to it now. A few years ago, I looked up her profile, where she's minimized her description to the term *bon vivant*. No employer, no profession. Her entire job history is erased. Which is fine. I don't begrudge her. It's been seven years, and I don't dwell on it, the space that grew between us. I've removed all the doors and knocked out the walls so at least it won't get repeated.

I've seen that she's spending her new money well. She's posted a complaint that the feminine version—*bonne vivante*—isn't a thing. Unencumbered indulgence isn't so feminine. People are apprehensive about a woman's immoderation, her lack of inhibition. In her post, she complained about battling her own instincts, a impulse toward restraint she didn't know she even had, along with a selfie in a cathedral-like setting, raising a glass over an ornate presentation of glazed fowls and peppered yams, surrounded by accomplished revelers—the composer of an opera about an Israeli prime minister, a renowned illustrator of artful depravities, a celebrity chef with a fast-moving food truck, and Beau Bram.

"As if there is something better I should be doing?" she wrote online for anyone to read. "A bon vivant is a jolly *fellow*. Women aren't jolly, or at least we're not supposed to be. And believe me, there are plenty—*plenty*—of good reasons why."

She's become a character out of a Beau Bram novel, maybe even inspired one—a well-heeled swell poised for a takedown, on a collision course with her own delusions, believing her neighbors disagreeable and the voices in her head the worst of threats.

But I wish her well. I am happy for her, relieved she's in a safe, protected place. Pleased, even, that she's better off than me.

Below my windows, the flow is mostly downhill, mostly office workers managing the slope in heels and stiff shoes, racing to get where they're going. Some days the loudest noise I hear is a hard-sole shoe landing flat on the sidewalk, trying to keep from falling too fast.

CHAPTER SIX

MY DESK IS A thin board on a pair of narrow trestles, a style that's in line with the beams and boards in the rest of the apartment, stripped down, cleaned out, simple and efficient. The windows above it rattle easily enough. All it takes is a fairly basic explosion somewhere nearby, and there's wood rattling against wood, and dirt and dust, whatever's lodged in the rafters, comes sprinkling down, too. It's been this way since I tried remodeling. Losing a few walls loosened everything up. A window pane once shattered with just the tap of my pen. Just fidgeting, nothing forceful, on a morning of pacing. In a million pieces, the glass fell like a waterfall, a shimmering shower onto the sidewalk below.

I was lucky to miss the stream of office workers, though several shouted up when it hit the ground and sprayed out in front of them. "What the…" "C'mon, man…" But no one really slowed, just a new steady crunching, like soldiers in formation on a practice field.

"Sorry…so sorry…" I tried yelling down. "Watch it. Watch your step, please…" I was mortified. I had to wonder what they thought of me, and of this building falling apart, crumbling right in front of them, turning their commute into an obstacle course. But the crunching continued. No one stopped to clean it up or kick shards to the curb or clear a path for others. No one waited to see if I was okay.

A young fellow took two steps into the breakage, took the time to check the soles on his nicely buffed boots, and pushed his wireless headphones deep into place. Everyone has their own business and keeps their nose in it. I stuck my hand through the open space and felt the breeze come straight at me.

The window was easy to fix. A couple clicks is all it took: the people who send Lennon with my regular deliveries offer a selection of other services, too, a curated directory of craftspeople and technicians who can unclog a toilet, unscrew a light bulb, or undo a pounded a nail. Problems are solved with seamless interactions. Emergencies dissolve in the most on-demand way, like a fire hose always at full pressure. In under an hour, Devan came knocking in a crisp new tool belt, confirming my name and my trouble before heading to the open window.

It was thrilling to watch him take out his tools, a cat's paw and a hammer. It reminded me of my remodeling work, having the walls down, opening everything up. Devan pierced the frame's paint and the trim splintered free. I leaned in beside him and saw brownish rope and thick weights exposed in wood casing. A simple, reliable system hidden in there, one I hadn't found myself. He worked quickly, but paused and stepped back to give me some space. I grinned at him, he sort of smiled back. The app promised he'd return the busted window by the end of the day.

"Wait," I told him as he hoisted the frame. "What happens next? Where are you taking that?" A workshop, a collective. I wasn't sure. Maybe he only does removals and delivers it to someone else, a specialist, a glazier, someone with the right skills. It was a nice enough day; I could live with a missing window. But I wanted some assurance my window would come back.

He rested the frame on his waist and recited the procedure. "I have a shop a few blocks away. I'll take the frame there, cut the glass, glaze it, then bring it back to re-hang it." He made it sound simple. Like I was an idiot for slowing him down.

"There's a workshop in the neighborhood? I had no idea."

"What do you mean?" For a beat or two, we looked at each other, confused. I thought I knew my streets well. He seemed surprised I didn't. "You don't recognize me?" he quizzed me. "I walk by here with my girlfriend all the time. We were both at the last library meeting." Then his look turned offended. Like this was about something else now. A pretty routine repair was starting to get weird. "You know this won't be cheap, right?"

"Of course, of course." I shook my head, trying to acknowledge every wrong thing I must've implied. "But this works, the app, the network? Everything as advertised?"

"Pretty well," he said. "I get a steady stream of customers." He readjusted the weight, still trying to look patient.

"It's just that..." I started, "I'm embarrassed I don't know how to fix this myself."

I watched him try to smile, but I was obviously keeping him, and now it felt like he was trapped there, like he needed to be dismissed. I tried one more time:

"You know how nobody works with their hands anymore but everybody talks about how much they want to?"

"Everybody?" he said, and took the opportunity to head for the door. "I do other things, too. I'm in a band. We tour. My girlfriend does sculpture. I help her out with that. I have buddies who bartend, and I fill in now and then."

I was nodding my head even with his back to me. This hadn't gone well, and I don't know how rewind. Stories like his are intimidating anyway: a man on the move looking in different directions, always game for whatever's next. The short list he rattled off is a lot more than I can claim, more than I've done my entire working life, a big chunk of which has been spent at this desk, looking out through the window that's under his arm, getting carted away.

"A boat is the next big thing. Fix something up. Sail around Mexico." He was already outside, headed down the stairs, as if he expected me to keep following.

"Mexico," I told him, and I was confused again. Because it seemed like a small ask, not a next big thing, like he wouldn't even need a boat for that. He could get in a car and be there in a day. I'd never been, but Mexico seemed manageable, maybe not such a big deal. I followed but stopped at the top of the stairs.

I wasn't gauging Devan right, and I'd turned this easy window repair into something awkward and weird. So I kept it to myself, what I imagined for him, where he'd come from, where he was going: Several years ago he probably picked up a popular memoir, a story about discovering the value of skilled labor, probably a lot like the one that had crossed my desk, championed by my man in St. Louis, along with myself. It was part of a trend marking a renaissance in the trades, and at the time, it made a lot of noise, a lot of folks talked about it, arriving with a wave of digital burnouts. The author appeared in a lot of different flannel on a lot of different talk shows. St. Louis and I liked what we saw, joined in with the trend, and published a slim volume on the spiritual aspects of working with wood. The central example was a man who made owls—made a career out of owls—using a fairly basic jigsaw. He ditched his relentless CFO job track and ended up spending longer days and hours behind safety goggles, thinking about god, than he ever did in mergers and acquisitions. Our book had a narrow focus but also real depth, assigning soulful potential to muscles and bones, elevating the synaptic connections that come with repetitive work to the level of spiritual ritual. I thought it was all extremely seductive—and then the next thing was happening, a new book was calling, and I had to keep moving. A collection on butchering trends in central Copenhagen was pulling our attention then—followed by lining up new puppies for the year ahead.

Someone like Devan, I suppose he latched onto the heady romance of it too, but very unlike me, actually ran with it. He lived the life, made the dream, working when he wanted, coming and going as he liked. The app I used to find him was especially slick: he only talked to his clients when it suited him, when he wanted to. He could've come and gone here without a word. He could've easily never mentioned that I'd ignored him for years.

Inside, I waved my hand through the space with the missing glass. It felt like a sudden nothing, with the air through my fingers. A few hours later, Devan returned as scheduled. I met him at the door, gave him his space, and tapped on five stars before he even left.

But that wasn't the last one. When the second window broke, there was no shattering cascade. It was a gunshot that left a small round beveled space. It must've come in the night. I didn't hear the shot and couldn't find where it landed. I searched several times, scanning the walls, lining up the trajectory, trying to figure out where it had come from and where it had gone. The glass was otherwise intact, so I thought I could leave it. But on some days, especially wet ones, a column of cold air shot straight through. Plus, the optics weren't good. A place with bullet holes is not the kind of place I wanted to believe I lived in.

The kind of place I lived in was supposed to be magic. A leafy, quiet break from the hustle down the hill, the contrast is dramatic, it always has been. Once you've climbed the first block, you arrive on our corner and feel different, calmer, like you can maybe take a breath and find your own pace.

There used to be regular gunfire. I used to hear more sirens, too. When Sylvie and I first arrived, we'd lie in bed and listen for it. Not a lot of street noise made it up the hill, the trees and buildings shielding us, but we'd lie there and whisper about what we'd gotten into.

"Was this is a bad idea?" Sylvie wondered in the dark. "What the hell are we doing here?"

I didn't know for sure. "Maybe we're just hearing backfire." I used to say that a lot, and we'd wait under the covers for police sirens to follow. It was Sylvie who pointed out what we were doing, staying up late to listen for our neighbors being violent.

"Is this really happening?" she'd say through the dark. "People raise kids here? Is everybody in bed thinking the same thing right now?"

I knew what she was thinking, and I knew who she was thinking about: Maggie, who'd move here because of the edgy mix, the fixer-upper vibe, a neighborhood being nurtured, which seemed to fit with raising a child. She would've heard the same gunfire, would've waited for the sirens. She would've turned to her husband and had the same talk.

I knew it was about Maggie because our own talk was dropping off. Getting pregnant wasn't happening. We hadn't started trying, and neither one of us acted with the right plans in mind. We hadn't budged since we moved here, never moved toward the parent track, even though the apartment was supposed to be the first step. Even as Maggie came and went, we were still finding our way, and the kid across the street didn't help much. If that's what children were like here, how could we do any better? Then other signs followed: We lashed out at double-parkers at the library's story time, and we'd get real petty about the growing number of strollers. The children we weren't having became part of the list, one more latent annoyance, another justifier for our irritation with each other.

"How is she doing?" I tried asking Sylvie. "Does Maggie like being a parent? Are they settling okay?" I didn't know then that the neighbor kid was harassing her. I just knew Sylvie crossed paths with her now and then.

"Really?" Sylvie told me. "Just stop it. Please."

"What? Stop what?" I couldn't see her in the dark. We'd just heard a siren. We were waiting for more.

"Stop talking to me like I'm your local translator. Like I'm your guide to the outside world." Beside me, I could see her waving her arms in the dark, as if she were swatting at everything I was missing.

"What? I don't do that…"

I felt the covers pull her way. She scoffed into her pillow. "Have you ever tried talking to Maggie yourself? You know they moved in over a year ago. I think they might be *settled*. My god…do you have any real interest in what's happening around here?"

I could feel her go tense, hear her muffled breathing.

"Sylvie," I said, "I'm just trying to be neighborly." I said it real gentle, trying not to sound defensive. I thought I being was considerate, asking about people she cared about. All our bickering aside, I've never thought of myself as the type who kept his head buried. But back then especially, I was spending more time with the queue, watching what people sent us, keeping tabs on the business and projects coming our way.

I couldn't convince her. She didn't find my work compelling— everyone in her office worked as hard as I did, everyone she knew could claim their career was all-absorbing. The books we produced didn't seem to impress her or qualify as a serious distraction. This, too, made it onto the complaints list, the very separate worlds we weren't sharing with each other. And one more thing: I think she resented my work-at-home setup, never imagining I might envy the commuter stream on the sidewalk, all those people who had somewhere else to go. The way the list was going, with or without bullet holes, this wasn't a place to bring a child into.

I was relieved when Devan showed up again to fix it. "Really appreciate your coming back," I told him and kept my distance.

"I'm your closest guy. Down the street, remember?" He hoisted the frame again and made for the door. "I go where the app tells me to go."

He brought it back the same day. I kept my distance while he worked, and I dreaded having to rely on him again.

When the third window broke, the glass fell inside following a thick paving brick. I don't know who tossed it. I was watching when it happened. Sylvie would've pinned it on the kid across the street, but it was long after he left—long after she left, too—so I had to guess on my own, with the wind blowing even harder through the broken space.

I called St. Louis straight off. I told him my day was wrecked. He tried to tell me it was bigger than just a day ruined. "Who do you think did it? And what were they thinking? Who thinks you deserve a brick through your window?"

I already know I'm not aware of the way people see me—my pacing, my ranting. I'm a sitting duck for a bully with a strong throwing arm. The old woman from the library mistook me for a newcomer, confusing me with the neighborhood's fancy upgrades, thinking I took advantage of the evictions and displacements.

But it could also be random, like the glue in our locks when Sylvie was still here. There was no note, no one claiming responsibility, and no one following up with accusations. To me, that meant they wanted to be anonymous and, maybe, just maybe, they didn't know me either. It could've been anybody, any of the throngs walking by. Maybe not the office workers, but the stragglers, the tourists, the juggling clowns trudging uphill now and then. I can never be sure who's packing a paving brick.

So I replied to St. Louis, "Let's not make it a big deal. Nobody got hurt. Vandalism happens. I know a guy who can fix it in an hour."

But it took more than an hour, and it wasn't Devan. When I searched online, his local shop wasn't listed, and when I used the same app service, they sent another man, older, with an accent I couldn't place. He showed up late, made a big spread of his tools, and advised me it would take up to a week to get it fixed and back in place.

"A week?" I told him. "Is there a backlog or something? How many windows are getting hit by flying bricks? Is that the kind of city we're living in now?"

The repairman bowed his head. He set his tools down for a minute. Maybe he didn't understand me. It took him a while, but he came round to responding, and it was clear he had a hard time assembling the right words. "There weren't a lot of windows last time I was at my home. *Anywhere*," he added, and he used a gruff tone, like mine was hurtful, like he knew of many places, many homes, many living situations in worse shape than this. He put me in my place. I knew what he was saying. I watched him expose the window's rope and weights, and I stayed out of his way, staying mum till he left.

Someone else, a much younger man with an Alabama accent, returned the repaired window on time the next week.

"Crap," I told him, "I was hoping to apologize to the guy who took it out."

"For what?" he asked, but set straight to work. It was my third broken window, real evidence of real danger, but also something I could fix with a phone call again. I wasn't sure how much frustration I was supposed to feel. St. Louis thought I wasn't outraged enough, a part of me wanted to apologize for complaining at all, and the young man from Alabama backed off when I offered a tip.

The fourth window was smashed with a large-format picture book, a coffee table edition hurled by an agitated reader. *Howl: A Furry Fantasia* told the region's history from the perspective of crafty pups, the kind that stand upright and wear funny hats—a book that would quickly morph into the calendars we've come to depend on year in, year out. It all started as a modest picture-less book, a series of love letters that would describe historical turning points within the details of the puppies' adoration for each other. But as it evolved into an annual calendar, we were faced with making things cute. Kate, our promotions director, pushed hard for this, taking it on as her first project and seeing the potential for significant historical perspectives twinned to the marketability of furry wet noses.

In the beginning, as a book, the project was delivered chapter by chapter, and at each step new complexities arose. Two Portuguese Water Dogs were assigned to depict the early Mission settlements— one a Franciscan monk, the other an Ohlone squaw, the object of his affection. The arrangement, the book's first one, almost sunk the whole project, deviating broadly from what we expected. Although we were forced to admit to greenlighting the idea, we quickly saw our mistake, signing off on the depiction of brutal subjugation as a cuddly romance. I consulted St. Louis. He put Kate on the revisions. From her office in New York, she worked closely with the author in her Kansas City living room using long video sessions to revise the text.

But problems persisted. More histories arrived perverted. The project kept delivering unexpected insults. Gold rush forty-niners were delegated to French Bulldogs, both with old-timey goggles and cheeky kerchiefs. The problem here was the lack of gender distinction, confusing the love letters printed alongside them. It was an interesting mixed message, but Helen, the author, was revolted. Again, Kate stepped in to handhold the revisions.

Two earthquake survivors, a red-eyed bloodhound and a Pomeranian fluffball, had genuine appeal. They seemed to transcend conventional boundaries in a way that recalled Montagues and Capulets.

The odds seemed stacked against such a pair; with the city fallen around them, you root for them in their own corner of heaven. All four of us—Kate, Helen, St. Louis, and myself—agreed we could live with this one.

For a spread devoted to gay liberation, Helen dressed a rowdy crowd of Dachshunds with leather and boas. The love letters here pined for equality but also needed some editing, and some trimming to accommodate a PG rating.

In a counterintuitive move, dear Helen chose two muscular Rottweilers for hippies, representatives of free love that seemed awkward and disinterested. The large breed looked too square for pot and polyamory. I didn't buy it either. I took this one on myself and suggested scruffy mutts. The revised photo was propped with daisies and hookah pipes, but the project's expenses were mounting. We expected to lose our shirts, a genuine discouragement at this early stage.

None of it was inspired. No new ground was broken. The book was ending up far from its original vision, now a series of mild-mannered glossy entertainments that concluded with Bichon Frises in thick-rimmed glasses nose to nose on a pile of tiny digital devices.

It was the kind of project I vowed never to repeat. The backlash was vicious and demoralizing. Serious booksellers scoffed at early galleys. Reviewers ignored it. A few indie blogs caught wind and launched nasty diatribes against our new publishing initiative, asking if the world needed more offenses like this. Right out of the gate we were called irresponsible, negligent in our role as cultural gatekeepers and ridiculous to fancy ourselves relevant. For a couple of weeks, we were a punching bag for those alert enough to notice.

Dark days followed. I was inconsolable. I sat at my desk and scrolled through the puppy pics, none of which looked cute now or even much like dogs in love. Whole days were consumed in spirals of panic. I don't remember sleeping. At one point, Sylvie noticed, and when she peeked over my shoulder, she laughed at the screen. "Whatever that is, it's got to be a joke."

St. Louis called regularly, trying to put the best spin on things, and when the first numbers came in, no one knew what to say. The snarky denunciations peaked fast and early—only to be surpassed by skyrocketing popularity. The book flew off shelves. Our *Howl* was a hit. We worked like mad to keep up with the demand.

Suddenly we had success, at least of a certain measure. We were sitting on a goldmine—we just weren't digging it right. In those early days, when the first numbers were coming, that was when a copy was hurled through my fourth window. Across the cover, "#notwelcome" was scrawled in neon green spray paint, right over the puppies arranged in a group photo. An extreme form of criticism. A direct hit on our ambitions. Right when we couldn't print enough to keep pace.

The next several weeks swung between mass frenzy and serious calls to shut down. We'd committed crimes of cultural appropriation that infuriated scores of influencers and columnists—but it was also a book that thousands clearly loved, enough to plunk down thirty bucks and tell their friends to do the same. We'd made a mess of history, and lots of folks were delighted.

I didn't know what our next move should be. St. Louis arranged a summit with me, him, and Kate, who had done her best and was somehow still smiling. On the call, she kept pushing: "Maybe we all need reminding: We're not a nonprofit. We're not supported by a university. Our objective, our business, is to make money—"

"Of course," I interrupted.

"—and a book like this can pay the bills for many others."

I knew what she was saying, but that argument wasn't enough. "The only books it will pay for are more just like it. We've made a mark with these puppies. People know us by this one. Is that all we want to do? Produce more furry affronts? How do we feel about the people we're pissing off?"

St. Louis stepped in, sensible as ever. "I think we can course correct. We'll just do a lot better. Re-devote to core values. Show our true colors."

I nodded along with him. "Redouble our commitment to the unexpectedly overlooked."

"The unexpectedly overlooked," St. Louis echoed.

"And, you know… maybe, also… find a middle way," Kate said and went on to map our future, advocating for the calendar alternative, spinning the book into a lucrative annual but stripped of its controversy and any ties to us. "A happy secret cash cow. It almost sounds like magic."

Kate was young, fresh out of Howard, whip-smart, blonde Afro-ed, and remarkably joyous-minded. She was looking to make her mark in media. She was also delightful daily, without fail, any time we had the opportunity to talk.

She came to us as magazines were consolidating, and Kate was jumping from one to another like lily pads on a watery idyll, unfazed by the compromises, uninhibited by the glamour, pivoting swiftly between mastheads even as they were slimming. From cooking journals to political rags to fashion news sites, she always knew the next launch, the next collapse, and the next fraught merger. She was already known as a skilled fixer, a deep well of resources. Her byline was ubiquitous, her time was in demand, and her tenure with us was quickly transformational.

She stayed in New York, essentially making us bicoastal, with bragging points for an outpost in St. Louis. It took a while to master, to find the right workflow, which came to mean Kate and I never occupied the same room.

"How are you, dear darling?" she would begin our video chats. I noticed her affecting a slight Caribbean accent. I never knew her connection there. Her CV listed a childhood in Philadelphia. "So much cheery sunshine on our agenda today."

I used to dress up for her, or at least tidy myself more than usual, and I'd schedule our calls after Sylvie was at work, making sure she wouldn't hear the tone Kate brought to the table.

"Look at you." She leaned close to the screen. "You're sweet to run a comb through your hair."

I appreciated that she noticed. "I like the way you think, Kate. Just trying to keep up." And then we'd dedicate a little time to these undisturbed assessments, grinning at each other, pleased by our connection, enthralled by our two-person mutual admiration club.

"I'm going to need you to budge a bit, darling. Work with me on the brand. Meet some people on your coast. Other editors. Cultural programmers. That sort of thing." Then she'd look at the camera like a vanity mirror, touching up her hair and straightening her collar. "Just a short list of people I think you should meet."

It was never outright flirting, but it was deeply flattering having someone so current, so connected, so in-the-right-groove showing up on my screen and engaging with our work. I never really got over it. It always felt generous, validating. Every conversation, it felt like the cusp of something big.

Of course, that's her job. That's why she pulls a paycheck. Not to make me feel special, but something much harder: to take experiences of substance and turn them into shiny mirrors, adding thrill and buzz beyond their own words. She packages our books with acumen and seduction, with flair and deep feeling, wrangling designers and finessing jacket copy. They are standouts on store tables. They glow in shop windows.

For a difficult book from Niger, the illustrations looked touchable. For a fictional memoir of Lady Bird Johnson, the cover's calligraphy was deeply emotional. Launch parties reeked of high-end extravagance even though they were thrown together quickly on a dime. She directed short films that doubled as promotions, and she showed up at book fairs eager and engaged, the opposite of exhausted.

Without Kate, there are only words on ragged margins. She elevates them to touchstones and social inflections, wrapping them up like the most thoughtful gifts and then maneuvering them into the right cultural moments. There is a multidimensional mastery to her work, without ever letting us see her sweat.

"I'm nothing without you, darling," she'd tell me.

"Right back at you," I'd say and try to sit up straight.

But even as her skills expanded and her skills proved real, she started to slip in unexpected ways. We started talking more, revealing more of ourselves. I told her about Sylvie and our San Francisco neighborhood, and she reported the latest oddities of New York, the fitness trends, the juicing fads, the newfangled practices in spirituality that took on needless pretzel shapes. She never talked about dating, until a particular hockey player.

"Concussion sports, darling. They're not what you'd think."

I was excited for her and honored that she'd share another glimpse into her life away from our work. "Concussion sports," I repeated back to her. "What exactly am I supposed to think?"

"Injuries. Brain damage. Undiagnosed mood swings." She rolled her eyes and stuck her tongue in her cheek. "Football players who go on killing sprees." That was kind of a jolt. Not the talk I was expecting. I was thinking more along the lines of engagements, romance, major life events. "But I think they're sold short," Kate went on. "They actually have some interesting ideas. They move in different circles, and a lot of times, they come up with different ways of thinking about things."

"Okay…" I said. "I think I'm following." I moved to my seat's edge. I was intrigued by her enthusiasm. I was ready to go wherever she was going. Whatever she'd found fascinating would go double for me.

"Just last night, we're talking about science and institutions and how we see the world around us. We were out for Indonesian. They don't have much of that back in Saskatchewan."

"Lots of prairie out there. I love where this is going."

But then I didn't. Not at all. What followed was a shock. A monumental floor drop. Without stutter or apology, in her fearless pleasant way, she explained her new interest in Flat Earth theories and that we can't really be sure about our planet's real shape.

"I just don't know," she told me. "How can we be sure? I mean, *really* sure?"

I didn't know where to begin: photos from space, ancient astronomy, geology, geometry, generations of explorers with and without advanced degrees. "But we can," I said to her. "We can be sure." I paused for a moment. "Yes, we can be sure the world is round." I think back on that exchange, I play it over and over, and I'm convinced even now my bafflement was clear.

"And what about other planets? What about the moon? Maybe it's just as flat." She didn't seem to hear me. "Everything else circling around us could be just as flat. I mean, how do we know that for sure?"

"Moon aside, I don't think much else is circling around us—"

"But you get what I'm saying…"

"No. I really don't."

"Anyway," she said, ready to move on. "That's what we've been talking about. Lots of talking and talking. And it's bringing us closer and closer every minute of every day."

"So you're serious. You're not kidding."

She smiled at me and squinted close at her video screen. "Peter moves in different circles. It's been really eye-opening. It's remarkable to get exposed to a new world of ideas." And she kept on smiling, like it was just so simple.

"But it's not," I told her. "The Earth's not flat, Kate." And because the next thing I'd say would be deeply hurtful, I stopped myself short.

"Peter calls it 'dimensional doubt.' The willingness to challenge everything from every angle."

I didn't know who I was talking to. It was like my lungs had been stolen, along with my vision. The rest of that meeting went in fits and starts, and I let Kate do the talking, hoping she'd stop and say it was just a joke. That she'd cackle and move on, delighted to shake me up. But that didn't happen, and the longer it didn't, the less I could keep up. It felt like a betrayal, like a deep breach of trust. I immediately doubted her work, her every decision. We all have our blind spots. But this was too much.

It was like talking to a stranger, who'd also been a close advisor, and who turned out to believe in medieval bloodletting. We finished our meeting, and I mostly nodded and agreed to the items on our agenda—a small book tour upstate and a booth booked at a Florida fair—and then moved to quit the call so I could consult with St. Louis.

"I can't work with her," I told him. "If she's really so malleable, so open to suggestion, I don't think we should trust her handling our work."

He also needed a minute to let it sink in. "She really said that? She wasn't joking?" he asked. "But we need her. She makes our stuff sell."

I hit mute and rocked back and forth, head in my hands, trying to grasp the weight of Kate's unraveling. To figure out how we could replace her and what it would mean for our books and our business.

"I'm not sure she's unraveling, if that's what you're thinking." St. Louis tapped on his screen, trying to get me back. "She's in love. She's sort of young. We've all been through that phase. Those years where we have to question everything.—"

"She's in love…?" I said. "Is that what you'd call it?" I was ready for answers, any decent explanation, and I watched him try to back-pedal, apologizing and searching, looking for another parallel, a better example. I watched him scramble in his head—St. Louis, my rock, my sounding board, my touchstone of the sensible, stumped by the baloney of interplanetary flatness.

"Let's assume it's not a big deal. It's just a casual conspiracy." The light came back in his eyes, and he looked fully convinced. "People think conspiracies are interesting these days. Doesn't matter what they're actually about. Like the one that says we're all in a hologram, and our world is a simulation run on some distant program. This is probably in line with nutty stuff like that."

I didn't get the connection. It was beyond my comprehension. I worried for her stability. I thought she could self-destruct. Maybe we were putting too much on her, raising her to a role she wasn't ready for yet.

Then St. Louis suggested a tidy solution, a go-between arrangement. He'd deal with her and work as our middleman, keeping a close eye on misguided Kate. "This could work," he assured me. "You're on different coasts. You never truly interact. We can send her our books, she'll whip them into beautiful things people will pay money for, and same as ever, you'll witness the results with your jaw hanging loose."

"But she's crazy…" I tell him.

"I'll take care of her," he said, and I never suffered another meeting with Kate. We eased into the arrangement and started a new workflow. I made myself unavailable, and with no specifics spelled out, St. Louis stepped in as an essential interlocutor. Now he and I work more closely than ever, and then he ships our work to Kate, who guides them through her alternative universe into a bustling media landscape.

It's not easy to rely on someone I don't trust, a partner who brings both brilliance and nonsense. But it was her idea to keep the puppy calendars going, the kind of compromise that keeps me focused on the exceptionally overlooked. My bond with St. Louis is equally buttressed. A broken window has never delivered so much.

The fifth window broke all on its own, from pure rot. The wood frame had gone bad. It just fell from exhaustion, the trim turned to mush, unable to hold up its original weight. A few splinters flew. Mostly it was decomposed. Decayed from overuse and overexposure, too much neglect and benign abuse.

I was in the kitchen putting away Lennon's boxes, which even then were coming at a steady flow, way too much to stay on top of. Some days they got thrown out, going straight to the trash. My back was turned when I heard the window shatter. I rushed over and tried to catch the perpetrator, if someone were still out there. Another book, another bullet—but all I saw was rotten wood, Outside, Kenny and Darrel were attached at the waist, oblivious in their love bubble.

Now when I look up, I know what I'm looking through. Everything here has been broken already. Everything has already been replaced.

CHAPTER SEVEN

Dear Publisher:

I have written a book. An engineering memoir, based on my travels around the world to locations soon to be covered with rising oceans. The book describes futuristic solutions that probably won't seem so futuristic very soon.

It is a mix, documenting threatened lives as well as schematics of dykes, levies, canals, locks, and systems of reclamation.

Numerous themes are explored throughout.

I thank you for your timely consideration.

Sincerely,

The sketches are handsome, worth a book of their own. I was captivated before I got distracted by Beau Bram. This underwater book is the kind we're always looking for. Appealingly truthful. Creatively investigatory. But something is off. I'm still distracted. We're in a green-lit stride here, with all systems go—the history of the spleen is still picking up speed, a bestselling author is actually pitching *us*, business is steady despite a few sideshows—but I keep looking up, checking the sidewalk, feeling like all of it could go off the rails. Like we're due for a toppling, down a big peg or two. It is midmorning, the commuter rush has passed, and the fog has burned off.

I should be focused on Bram, finishing his manuscript. I've only got the last fifty pages or so. I should be reading and scrolling and posting notes in the margin. His story is tight. It moves with precision. But I'm still put off, nagged by the indifference, the neighbors who don't answer in the middle of the night.

In the last several pages, online fundraising pays the ransom, Danny is returned from the kidnappers, and the perpetrators are left to walk free. The incident is resolved within forty-eight hours, the kind of swiftness both the press and the police find unprecedented. In Christian's calls for help, their coupledom, their love bubble, is part of his message, insisting their life is as normal, as valuable, as agreed-upon as any. And once Danny is returned and the couple is reunited, posing for photos on their white Soho stoop, the blowback comes just as quick. The city is furious: Londoners want justice. They're disgusted by the protection the couple can crowd-raise. With all the attention and money, the actual crime, Danny's nightmare kidnapping, gets pushed to the side. People resent the speed of it, how quickly people rallied, the sympathy too easy, especially when the thugs are still at large and everyone else is left at risk.

"What are we supposed to do?" Christian responds, the couple's designated spokesperson. "Who wouldn't take advantage of every opportunity? Aren't we all responsible for protecting our loved ones?"

The controversy takes a toll. Christian and Danny end up fighting, and the public discussion gets between them like a wedge. It was only two days, but in his calls for help, Christian shared too many details, at least more than Danny would've liked; in an interview with a reporter, Danny formally forgives his captors, which is something Christian doesn't support. Their trust erodes, and they have to hide their breakup, so as not to enrage their critics even more. What started as a portrait of swells on the town becomes a cautionary tale of an intimate relationship getting tested by a community falling short.

Bram handles it all deftly—the characters, the settings, the tension, the erosion. Except for their closest neighbors, the public's reaction is made to sound reasonable. By the end, I feel like I understand what London is thinking. Things get out of whack when someone has too much influence. But there's still that moment in the first few pages, in the middle of the night, the desperate knock at the door, when no one answers a familiar voice begging. It's a small thing, a minor passage. But it's the first time I've ever felt that way about Bram's work.

It's early enough for steady traffic below. Office workers head downhill to the crossroads and buses. Plugged in, dressed up, focused on their own business. Lennon is piling into his EggSprout van, so I know what's waiting for me. I can tuck in today and stay focused on Bram's book.

In the vestibule, as I pick up Lennon's boxes, I hear rushing footsteps behind Kenny's door. I'm still there with my arms full as Kenny comes busting out. He's covered in sweat, and he's caught off guard finding me there. "Oh, thank god," he tells me, squeezing into the space with me. "I've got to get back to the hospital, but I can't find my phone or my wallet."

On reflex, I start searching my pockets, juggling Lennon's deliveries from one arm to the other. "Is Darrel okay? Something's gone wrong?"

Behind him, the door's still open, and I can see the set of stairs I've never really been up, I've only heard them race down. Uncovered wood treads, painted to look colorful, like the entrance to a home full of fun and love. But I'm still fumbling for my phone and starting to sweat a little.

Kenny is soaked through. Breathing hard, watching me, trying to be patient, always trying to be patient, shaking and even stomping a little now. I'm convinced I don't have it, then I find it in my front pocket. He grabs the phone from me and pushes me off it, all in the same jerky, sweaty move. We've maneuvered around the vestibule, and all on my own, I lose my footing, going backward, falling hard, and first losing the boxes, then falling some more. The tumble happens in pieces, covering several steps—I feel the blow on my neck, then my shoulder, my side and my knee, which gives a serious crack.

I can tell I'm all twisted, but then my vision narrows. I wouldn't call it focused, because it's not particularly clear, but from the sidewalk, from the base of our steps, I can see Kenny punching numbers on my phone, arguing with the call center. My vision slims down to him above me at the top of the climb, sweating and ranting, his T-shirt clinging and his volume increasing. He looks unhinged. Even I can grasp that.

"Kenny…" I call to him, and it takes another beat, probably searching for sirens, before he rushes down, racing to give the phone back to me. I look at him, then at the phone and then don't know what to do with either. It hurts to reach for anything, and as he watches me sort of stuck here, he tries to guide me back on my feet. But I don't think I'm ready. I can't get up yet. And Kenny's still breathing hard, still deep in his own emergency, trying to make room for some of mine now.

He rides with me in the ambulance, like he did with Darrel, and when the medics start with questions, I can answer for myself. I'm not so out of it. They ask what happened, and I tell them I slipped. At the ER, things are slow, so the intake is speedy, and once I'm in others' hands, in a bed with the curtain pulled, Kenny is off through swinging ER doors, disappearing down a brightly lit hall.

The next hours are blurred. The nurses serve up painkillers. My kneecap is either broken or bruised. I'm so high, so messed up, I'm not exactly sure, but several hours later I'm in the back of a cab, headed home. Just like that, about as fast as the fall happened. I have to hop up the stairs, juggling prescriptions and printouts of my rehab plan.

A hard plastic splint strapped with Velcro will keep my leg straight and extended for several weeks. I hobble to my desk with a stack of forms I don't remember acquiring, and when I glance at my screen there, Beau Bram's manuscript is still on it, blinking back at me.

It's already evening. The dusk skyline is purple, but here I am, back in my perch, as if everything is restored to where it should be. The cab driver has waited for some sign of safe landing. He waves at me from the street. The boxes from Lennon are also taken care of, neatly stacked just inside my front door.

Whatever just happened, I feel like I can take it. Like this isn't the worst or most devastating thing. I can get myself to bed, on top of the covers, even though half my body feels like it's somewhere else. The drugs make things fuzzy, but I can tell the pain is just under the surface. I caught a quick glimpse in the cab's rearview: my hair wrecked, my face ruddy and reddened, my shoulders stressed up around my ears. I do not look like a character from a Beau Bram novel. I am not a London swell, not even the neighbor of one. I look like a lot of people outside my window, not so much the commuter crowd, but more like a man who's been sleeping in the park up the street.

"Hello, stranger," Sylvie says, knocking as she comes through. "First thing tomorrow, we change your emergency contact."

I'm not sure if I've been dozing. But the room has gone dark, and I watch Sylvie stop short, both of us shocked by what we're seeing.

I lift my head from the pillow and swing my braced leg around.

"Don't do it," she tells me and puts a hand up. But she's also taking stock of what she's walked into. Last time she was here, I hadn't remodeled. There were walls and a door where she stands now, be-

tween her and me on the bed. This is the first time she's seen things
opened up. "Stay where you are," she says, looking up, down, everywhere. She pulls her shawl over her shoulders, then circles front to
back, hands out in front of her, like a cartoon blind person reaching
for something to trip her up.

I'm horrified she's here, that someone called and asked for her
help. And I'm embarrassed that I look like this, like I've been in a
gutter fight. I haven't imagined her here, in these rooms, in years. It
feels strange and out of time. But I'm also mortified I can't meet her
upright on my own two feet. "It's worse than it looks. It's just a deep
bruise. An accident on the front steps."

She stands by my desk and looks at me from there, hands on her
hips with the windows behind her. Then she pulls a low-slung chair
to my bedside, so we're toe to toe, with her trying to smile warmly,
like she's not worried in the least. She crosses her legs and from that
low vantage takes another troubled look around the open room.

"I'm sorry you're still my emergency contact. That's not deliberate."

She nods and sighs and takes a look at her phone. "I tried to get
to the ER, but you were already checked out. I was on this side of
town anyway. Across the street, actually."

"Across the street…"

She points behind her, in the direction of the women's building, and then I watch her look up again, lifting the phone to take
pictures, capturing the kitchen, the windows, the new long, open
sweep. She nods as she does, signaling approval. "Looks real nice in
here," she says from her chair, then swipes some sawdust from the
top of her shoes.

There's a tone, a new one, which I don't remember. Along with
the kind of shoes I never saw her in. The robe-dress she's wrapped in
is both sumptuous and easy, another surprise. Before, she was always
sophisticated but practical. Understated, streamlined. I never knew

her to dress sensually. But that's how she walks the streets around here now.

I lie back on my side, horizontal again, so I can at least see her from the bed. I'm numbed by the drugs—I wouldn't usually lie down when there are visitors in the house. But I have to give in here. The whole of Sylvie has shifted. She's stepped into a new persona, exuding wealth and high taste. I can't help it, but I appreciate her approval of my remodel. It means something extra, maybe because of her new status. With that tone, her new rank, I watch her pull her shawl tighter as her gaze returns to me.

"I'm glad you're okay. And doing so well." She gestures around.

"What's happening across the street?" I ask. It's still odd to be chatting, picking up from nowhere, and to be doing it all from bed, as if no time has passed and we're on a clean slate. But I smile at her anyway, through hazy mixed feelings, and she smiles back, tilting her head to meet mine. A nice, quiet moment. A pharmaceutical moment. Chemically engineered to be expectation-free.

"It would've been inhuman to not check on you." She takes another moment before she gets up. "So I'm here. You're good. I'll get out of your hair now."

I try to move, but she's already at the door. She seems relieved to leave without an incident. And once I'm left alone, with the room getting darker, I realize she's come and gone with nothing, empty-handed, with no assurance that my support networks are helping and no offer of her own. No questions about doctors or the extent of my injury. She seems comfortable walking away and closing the door behind her.

As the room darkens, there's still no word from Kenny. Which is also troubling. The last I saw him, he was pushing through the heavy ER doors. No check-in, no circle-back, no apology since I've come home. I only notice his absence after Sylvie comes and goes. I hadn't thought to expect him. I assumed he had his hands full; he was sweaty and distraught when we met this morning. Regardless, my fall wasn't his fault. He didn't do it on purpose. He must have Darrel and bigger things than my scraped knee on his plate.

I fade in and out, dehydrated and dizzy. Across the room, the morning's deliveries are still stacked by the door. I swing my leg off the bed and hop over to them. It will take a few trips to shuttle them to the kitchen, so I leave off midway, abandoning a few small ones like little hungry beggars in the middle of the room.

On my way back to bed, I catch a party of bridesmaids outside the windows, a gaggle of boas and princess tiaras in jeans and back-packs filled with open bottles. They are whooping and shouting and slurring their way through a Whitney Houston standard. In the dark, they take the climb at a fierce pace.

CHAPTER EIGHT

BEAU BRAM IS ON stage at a festival in England, an old country estate overrun with genteel ticketholders, an attractive, middle-aged crowd moving between food tents and curated performances. A white-wine scene facing a blustery afternoon with fashionable scarves and tailored overcoats. Clouds move like props above manicured gardens. A swooping video captures the atmospherics before fading to a stage on a broad green lawn, where an interviewer presses Bram on his next book.

"We're all waiting…" The interviewer scooches to the edge of his chair, high-backed as a throne, a basic shtick that earns a few chuckles. "You've won most of the major awards. Critics follow your choices closely. I'm sure other authors seek your advice, too."

"Other authors know better than to follow my advice," Bram says and shoots a grin. The video takes the opportunity to pause and insert more local color, a few seconds of hummingbirds on a stand of primroses. Prokofiev fills the background. When it fades back to the interview, something's been cut, some of the exchange on stage or maybe a question from the audience. Something is missing. It doesn't feel like we're picking up where we left off.

Bram has a microphone in his hand, and he's talking down to an unseen face in the crowd. "No, no, that's not right at all. You've completely misread my work." It's a serious shift. Someone's shouting from the crowd, and Bram is engaging them, though the camera and audio only capture him on the stage. "No, sir. No. My work really should not be called *confessional*."

The reply isn't audible and still off-camera, and I can't really guess what is being said. But Bram seems to be getting more and more agitated. He lifts the microphone, but the video cuts away again, to a ground-level sweep along a tidy blooming flowerbed. More violins, too. The jump is disturbing.

Cutting back to Bram, he is standing at the edge of the stage, one hand gripping the mic, the other buried in his pocket. He stands stiff and has a stern expression. "We're not going to get into that. Not now or any time. I just don't feel comfortable demanding that from readers. Others do, others can, and I admire them enormously. But I don't feel like I can responsibly put out work like that." A few more audience members have begun shouting back, joining the others' confrontation. I have never seen such a violent reaction from attendees at a literary event.

The video jumps again to the estate's gardens, a stand of lilies quivering in the breeze. The insertions are feeling aggressively surreal now, and when it's back again to the stage, the questioner has left his seat. He's trying to intercede, putting a hand on Bram's shoulder, who still faces down the audience. The author responds with a violent shrug.

When someone near the stage's edge holds a phone up to record this, Bram raises a hand over his face, then squats and tries to swipe it away—actually tries to grab the phone from the spectator-fan, all in one angry motion. "No, no, no," he's shouting. "See, this is something I hate." He points at the lens recording this video now. "Your photos are offensive. That's not what we're doing here."

"Bram—" The interviewer tries again. But the heckling from the audience is gaining momentum. The jeers aren't all discernable, but "phony," "fake," and "charlatan" are clear enough.

I have no idea what's happening. I found the video on a random search. It looks like a meltdown or a public mental collapse. I hadn't heard news of it. I had no idea Bram had experienced this.

"Let me just make this one point." Bram nods to a catcaller, then pauses to collect himself. "With the written word, we have ordered thoughts and structured arguments that enable analytic clarity. We have reflection and depth. The foundations of soulfulness, of understanding others. But if we rely on pictures, if we continue to become a purely visual culture—" He pauses to point at the phone he tried to swipe. "—listen, basically, if we only communicate with pics and selfies and crude cutesy icons, we're headed back to pre-Gutenberg times. We're communicating a lot like cavemen used to."

In the next cut, fluffy clouds race over the manor house, a steepled pile with long rows of high windows. We hear the native wind and the chirp of local birds. The mix is unrelentingly bizarre.

When we return to Bram, a man is climbing on stage and rushing the author, landing the first blow in a serious shoving match. The interviewer tries to keep them apart. Bram and his attacker are shouting obscenities. The video goes cockeyed as its operator jumps in.

It's a quick clip, and the video fades to gorgeous footage of waves crashing against a craggy shore, like something out of a PBS travelogue or the setting of a British bake-off.

When we cut back one last time, we're clearly at the beginning, with Bram and his interviewer in their original positions, seated opposite each other, sharing a polite laugh. They are in the middle of the event's early questions. The cut is out of sequence again. "Well, I'm going in a different direction with this one, Buck. Really starting from scratch."

"Interesting. You're the kind of author who can do whatever he wants, I suppose. I mean, you're that gifted. And I'm pretty sure your fans will follow wherever you go. I guess we'd be disappointed if you didn't do something entirely different..."

"What an awkward thing to say," Bram responds. "The most self-destructive thing I could do is to meet expectations..."

There are a handful of these videos, of Beau Bram on a rager, none of them so mixed up but always with the author on a tear, going off in response to a question or a comment, hair-trigger performances when his face goes red.

"America, this continent, is a goddamn powder keg, a thin crust of lies and cheerful deceit scaffolded over a panorama of hatred and fear, a shitload of despair just under the surface, inches below the purple mountains' majesty."

Whoa. I didn't know this side of Beau Bram. I had never seen him step out of the bestseller mold. Usually, he rounds out the portrait from his author photos, that salt-and-pepper bearded look that signals he's not going to and probably never has really lost control.

I look at the dates on the videos. The one from the summer shows a handful of outbursts, increasingly unhinged. There's also an interview with another author, a woman, who crows about Bram's eruptions. "He's become a volcano." She looks excited. "Finally, somebody's stopped being polite. Somebody's actually talking like we think."

But I'm not sure what to think. I don't think this bodes well. Another hitch in the proposal Bram has sent our way.

"I don't know either," St. Louis tells me. I've sent him links to the videos. "Maybe he's pissed off his regular editor. Maybe they see a loose cannon with too many liabilities, so they set him free..."

"Maybe," I say, but it's definitely a complication. As a rule, as a company, we're not so keen on public fuss—even if we agree with its substance. St. Louis shares my disgust with projects people send us, the vitriol, the disregard, the common lack of empathy—it's frightening sometimes. We don't like what we read in our fellow citizens' hearts. So we usually try to avoid confrontations like this.

There's the matter of style, too. I am not a fan of inflations. I don't like the smell of conspiracy rhetoric. The grandiose gets tired before it makes its point.

And Bram's outbursts, after watching several videos, they come off a little stagy. They look slightly practiced. I don't really believe they happened in the moment, off the top of his head, without at least some scripting and planning. I don't mean the footage of shrubbery or craggy shores. I don't know who that bit of razzle-dazzle belongs to. Maybe the event producers were stumped by what to do with him. But a handful of these videos capture a definite pattern. They can't all be spontaneous.

"I mean, come on," I say to St. Louis. "'*A thin crust of lies and cheerful deceit scaffolded over a panorama of hatred and fear.*' It has to be an act, a plot he's been hatching."

St. Louis taps on my screen, trying to direct my attention—we're doing one of our video calls, and I don't always remember I'm being broadcast. I've probably been ranting out the window again. "By the way," he tells me, "you look like hell today."

I'm sure I do. It's in the screen's reflection now. My face is still ruddy, my hair is still a wreck, and the drugs probably make my eyes look crazy. "Rough night," I tell him and promise details later, before quickly hanging up.

Beau Bram, on the other hand, is a portrait of vitality, a powerful presence in the photos posted by his publisher. Fit and calm. Not too young, not old. He's notorious for his drug history, years of speed and heroin and hiding in corners before a path to sobriety—a tolerable redemption, not too saccharine, and a story he told only once in an extended essay and to high critical acclaim. He quickly moved on to other things—his domestic fictions with their breathtaking turns—and it helps that he's unscarred, at least in photos and videos. You'd never guess he'd lived on the streets, used to dose regularly, or had any impediments to success at all. His handsomeness lends depth, anchoring the reader's trust. Of course I want to look past that, just like I believe he would, too.

But his pose, his head tilt, his enigmatic gaze when there's not the bright spark of his smile, his photos seem to shout a very clear message: he's the better man, the more careful observer, a builder of intricately mannered scenarios in the style of late nineteenth-century novels. Stories that move breath by breath, particle by particle, assigning corruption and betrayal to the subtlest detail.

"But sometimes," he says in his most recent video, "you just need to blow things up. Send things sideways, get deep-root unruly, upend everything in every manageable way."

I don't know what to think, if he's going through a phase or if this is all part of a series of staged spectacles. The videos don't sync with his words on the page.

I go back to his manuscript. Christian and Danny and a London divided. This is the book he is talking about in the video, the new direction he's headed, while screaming at the festival crowd.

The book isn't junk, but it's not his best either, and I'm still torn what to do with it. It's a gift, but a loaded one. I'm not sure a flawed thriller will be a good bet.

I'm still not 100% in my head yet—I need to remember that, because the pills are blurring my progression of thoughts. I lean into the screen, trying to flatten my hair in the reflection. But then I see Sylvie in the doorway behind me, stumbling, her bag open and the rest of her disheveled and out of sorts.

"Oh my god…" She's panting and panicked, twisting herself around, looking for tears or ripped seams. I wasn't expecting her. I thought it was clear how we'd left things yesterday. Her concerns are her own now, and they don't include me.

She's dressed in off-white, in a soft flowing pantsuit with another soft flowing shawl clutched tight across her shoulders, a cloud of pink and vanilla barely containing her heavy breathing and the sweat and tears across her face. I can see her knees are soiled, and her bag looks distressed. "Thank god you're home. I was just mugged—can you believe it? Some kid tried to attack me. Tried to rip my bag right off my shoulder."

I get up too quickly and end up back in my chair. The drugs are hitting me harder than they should. Sylvia crosses to me, dialing her phone as she comes, then talking into it immediately, describing what's happened to someone who is clearly not the police. She's using some rough language, rougher than she ever used around me.

"What?" I half-whisper. "I don't know how I missed that. I've been sitting right here…" I'm shocked by her assault—but also that she's back here, on this side of town, on my corner again. In seven years, I've never seen her back on our old hill.

She points to the building across the street and sort of mouths her answer—"lunch." But she's back to her lawyer or her city councilman, someone I can't identify on the phone. A friend who knows someone on the police force. She paces close to me, pausing to look out our windows.

She is ranting, raging with an anger I've never seen before—and then a large *boom* rocks the room, the windows, the whole house. She grabs my chair and looks outside. It's louder than the explosions Kenny and I have heard. Down the hill, a block away, it's the start of demolition. The first blow to a block getting cleared for the transit hub, a pharmacy chain crumbling to its foundations, shaking us as it goes.

I grab the desk as a stream of sawdust starts falling. Sylvie starts swearing, screaming into her phone. And then Kenny races in—Sylvie's left the door open—the first time he's seen me in my cast and on my pills. I have the spaced-out look of a sidewalk sleeper, the weathered and ruddy. I try to ward him off, but he leans in even closer. A second blast goes off. Kenny adds his own swears, Sylvie grabs the desk again, and more sawdust blankets the three of us.

"Hello there," I hear from the screen on my desk. I turn and see Beau Bram on a video chat. I don't know how it happened. I have no clue how it started, if I pushed the wrong button or clicked the wrong screen. But in the corner I can see the mess that I'm broadcasting, his view of me, Sylvie and Kenny yelling behind me, grabbing at furniture, trying to wave away clouds of sawdust.

"Just wanted to touch base," Bram tells me as he leans into his camera. He looks puzzled, trying to make sense of what he's looking at. "See what you're thinking. Hear what you need."

In the corner, I can see my own shell-shocked look, my fevered face and my hair on end, plus the duo behind me trying to greet each other.

Beau Bram pauses. He looks worried despite his upbeat tone. "I wanted to check in, see what you've got going, and how we can get you to the next level."

"What's happening?" Sylvie yells in her phone now. "Well of course I know where I am. I used to live in this shithole. But nothing like this ever happened here before."

When the third blast comes, the three of us are girded. It is not a total surprise, but it still shakes us up. The windows rattle. More dust falls.

Beau Bram shakes his screen, as if there's a malfunction. Then he continues with a conversation I haven't caught up to yet. "What I'm asking is, for you, what needs to change? When you look around, what do you see that's holding you back? I mean, I can see it. I can see it pretty clear. And maybe my book is part of that. Maybe it's not.

The point is, your trajectory is obvious, and I'd like to be part of it in whatever way I can."

I'm really not following, and I'm not even sure what he's talking about. "Listen," I tell him. I try to lean close, but I'm repulsed by my reflection, the yellow-white sawdust adding its own layer of crazy. "Can I call you back? It's an earthquake or something."

"I love it," Bram tells me and quickly disconnects, his head suddenly huge as he leans in for the click.

"Look at this fucking view," Sylvie says, leaning past me, oblivious to my call, holding her phone against her chest. "I still can't get over it."

"I will get this cleaned up," Kenny shouts from behind us, pointing to the sawdust, then dashing out the door. I can see him on the street below, flagging a car, speeding off again.

Sylvie pulls back and gives me another look, like she doesn't quite know what to make of me now. "I've got it under control," she says into her phone, straightening her hair in the reflection on my screen. "I shouldn't have burst in here," she says to me now. "This neighborhood…" But she stops herself. Shakes her head. Like she's not going to get into it. "So you know Beau Bram too?" she says almost breezily, before pulling the door closed behind her. I see her below, looking both ways, before jogging over to the building across the street.

I take a moment, still marveling at the sight of her, and a moment later I think I spot her on the top floor, behind the linen curtains in her billowy vanilla suit, regaling Max and Marleen in their corner window. The same one the kid used for his verbal assaults.

My heart rate is up, drilling through the pain meds. A horrible first impression—the worst—with Beau Bram. But what was that about? Why was he calling, and why was he talking like that?

"Beau Bram!" I report to St. Louis. "He just called. We just spoke."

"What the hell…?" I see him leaning in too, looking concerned. I still look pretty beat up, especially with the woodchip dusting. "What happened to you? You and I were just talking…"

"I don't think the book is what we think it is. And I think Bram wants more than a publishing contract."

Below, a couple arrives on the corner, unwrapping sandwiches from wax paper. A plaid thermos steams at their feet. I can't see what they're looking at. I don't have the same view. But they seem to be settling in, bringing their lunch to watch the demolition, the buildings falling flat a block down the hill.

CHAPTER NINE

THE BRACE ON MY knee isn't made for desk sitting, and watching Kenny run off again, I feel pretty helpless, like a bystander at a knife fight who trips on his own shoelaces, or a witness to a stick-up who walks into traffic and gets clocked by a cab. It's none of my business, I've never pried or even cared much. But things are different now. Kenny and I are more neighbor-like than ever. I'd like to know why he's always wired and manic, what he's always in a rush for. I don't even know where he was going when I fell. I know we're a long way from Christian and Danny's story—in fact, I know more about them than I do about Darrel—but we're connected, Kenny and I, by more than what falls through the cracks in his floor.

Off he went this morning, diving into another car, hitting his regular pace, the only one I've seen lately. No wave or nod. No friendly check-in. I still see Lennon down there, waiting it out like he often does, watching for Kenny to leave before climbing out of his EggSprout van.

Last night I cleaned up the sawdust before I fell into bed, fumbling with the vacuum while fighting my brace. The pills are still masking things, they keep me on edge. I feel more than a little frightened by what they're covering up. It's awkward to sit here, and I don't like to do it, but I Google Kenny now and spin through the results.

For Beau Bram, for authors, for people I work with, I search on-line regularly. It's okay and necessary. I need to know that someone who writes about the spleen isn't part of a criminal ring convicted of harvesting them. I should know if an engineer describing underwater marvels has a history of leaky dams or iffy sea walls. That's just good business, looking out for our readers. But for everyone else, with friends, with my neighbors, I depend on what happens face to face, what I can see for myself, from my windows, on the street, in a library basement. That's why my desk has stayed where it is. I think that's what Sylvie used to yell about, too.

As the search results line up, I see Kenny is a busy man. There's more than I suspected, even with his frantic pace.

He shifted careers five years ago—he's older than I'd guessed—and moved to a think tank-slash-advocacy group devoted to "distributive knowledge," a phrase that feels deliberately opaque. Could be anything. Could be nothing. Not the sort of description that inspires or delights.

Beyond the foundation's website, there's more interesting activity, a path more in line with his high-fright mode. One news item identifies him at a warehouse party the night of a massive fire. Another links him to a petty theft ring as a victim who's also a person of interest. A fundraising site lists a personal contribution to an immigrant relief group; another identifies him as a board member on a nonprofit tree farm. A news site quotes his opinions on the new hub under construction down the street.

I hadn't realized he was quotable, someone the media would turn to. He's a regular thought leader, an opinion-maker who just happened to watch me fall down the stairs this week.

I'm slow to type it, but I add Darrel to Kenny's search, taking a deep breath before scrolling the results. They both come up in a police report for one of their domestic disturbances. From that, I learn Darrel's last name, and from there…almost nothing. No details on his childhood or tough times in the Central Valley. No stories about his late husband or their friends in Dallas. There's not much digital evidence. No get-well messages or crowdfunding linked to his current hospital stay.

A real dead end around Darrel, and new confusion about Kenny. I haven't seen Darrel since the back of his ambulance, and I haven't seen Kenny running back up the stairs today. Crows come and go from the opposite corner, pecking at waxed paper left by the couple having lunch yesterday.

But from the building across the street, on the top floor, someone is waving, trying to get my attention. It's Marleen, Max's partner, the woman I met on the library's front steps. The glamorous private chef who couldn't stop staring at me. When I wave back, she lifts her leg and points to her knee, then points to mine. "You okay?" she says, mouthing the words. Her concern is genuinely surprising to me.

Then she holds up a dinner bowl. I can see steam rising. I can see it all the way over here. She points to it, then to me, then to herself, then to me again, nodding pretty fiercely. I nod back, appreciatively, and she's knocking at my door in a minute or less.

"I'm here. I'm here," Marleen says, pushing past me. She looks even smaller than at the library, blanketed now by a voluminous wool poncho dotted with oversized Aztec designs. She holds a large square Tupperware ahead of her, steadying it in both hands. "Sit, sit," she says and heads for my kitchen, taking in the place as she goes, stepping around abandoned EggSprout boxes. She sets the plastic on the counter, then starts through my cupboards, opening and closing most of them before finding what she needs: a giant soup bowl from Chinatown, a ladle, and a spoon.

She scuttles across the apartment, hurrying the soup past me and leading me back to my desk. She clears a space and slides the bowl a safe distance from my screens and papers.

"Sit," she says again, blowing on the bowl for me, then producing a small bag and a small bottle, both plastic, from under the poncho. She dumps them both in the soup, then gives it a swirl with my spoon. The steam seems to double and nearly fogs one of the windows.

It's a feast. Instant homeopathy. I can feel it moving through me, from my chest through my gut to my fingertips and toes, warming and expanding and circulating goodness, remarkable blood-borne assurance that all things will be glorious and fortuitous, now and forever after.

Marleen leans in for the first spoonfuls. She watches my reaction. "Thought so," she tells me and waves off my thanks. "I thought you needed that."

She inspects my prescription, picking up the bottle, squinting at the label. "Western shit," she says, but returns it to its place. "At least you're getting some. Good to have access. If this is the kind of relief you're looking for, I'm glad you can at least get your hands on it."

I turn around from my desk, bringing the soup with me. Marleen sits herself in the low-slung chair, still in the heavy poncho, and takes stock of my home. "Looks bigger from the inside," she tells me, nodding a little. "Spare but cozy. I get it, I get it."

I appreciate her assessment, but I'm still deep in the broth, still bringing to the surface all kinds of surprises, three kinds of meats and odd mini vegetables. "Soooo good," I tell her, shoveling, trembling.

She shrugs. "Been a while, right?"

I nod and shrug and have a feeling about our connection. I've seen Sylvie over there, and she would've said something, described me somehow, if not just as an ex-husband, especially after the mugging.

"But you're home a lot. You're a homebody," she tells me, leaning forward, inspecting my progress on the bowl.

"Chained to my desk," I finally say, but I always say that. "What about you? Home in the middle of the day?"

She smiles. "Mental health day. A little time off."

She seems in no rush, settling back in the chair. Then she sits up quick. "Do you have time to chat? Am I interrupting something? Do you have work you should be doing right now?"

I'm deep in the bowl again, taking in the steam, full-on slurping from the lip. I shake my head while I tongue at the last noodles. My head is still a mess, but my bones seem to loosen, and Beau Bram feels a million miles away. I much prefer Marleen, my new favorite person.

Marleen leans back, making herself comfortable. "So we've crossed paths with Sylvie." She pauses to smile at me, kind of shrugging, eyes rolling, like she's helpless about it, like these things just happen, the world is so small, with so many elephants in so many rooms, and there's really nothing much she can do about anything. "Our circles kept connecting. So it made sense to make time. You know, lunch or something." She suddenly reaches toward me, bridging the distance halfway, not so much to touch me but as if this must upset me, this talk about Sylvie. "Really lovely lady," she feels the need to tell me. "Really odd she used to live here, too."

"Really odd," I tell her.

"But isn't that how things happen? I mean, the best things, really. The right timing, the right people. Things happen around you, and you decide, finally, all right, let's do it. Let's make this baby happen."

I nod back at her, tuned to a slow fade, feeling my stomach settle, my muscles easing too. I could doze off right here if she weren't sitting so close, really craning at me, and so mindful, cautious, tiptoeing around something to do with my ex-wife. I feel like it's my turn, like I have to say something. "Sounds like you had a very good lunch."

"All three of us," she tells me. "Max and myself, and I think Sylvie too, we'd never felt the kind of connection we'd been feeling. We'd been meeting, talking, *plotting* for a while. It was nice to finally have her over to the house."

"I bet. Very nice." I want to be more engaged, I'd like to be a proper host, take the lead, talk us through this, really drill down on lunch, the infinite potential for steaming bowls of soup there, and what she means when she emphasizes *plots*. But my eyelids are getting heavy; I'm as comfortable as I've been since I fell down the steps.

It's nice to hear Sylvie's her name and confirm she's doing well, and it's swell we've even found people we like in common—I'm a little in love with Marleen at the moment, mostly her soup talents and, if I can rally for it, I'd like to hear what excites her, what she's passionate about, because she's moving to the edge of her seat now, needing to get close for what's coming next.

She's reaching my way again, tittering with excitement. "The baby," Marleen tells me. "She's the ideal third parent. We know our limits, what Max and I can handle. Having Sylvie commit, having her all in and on board, really makes all the difference. Between the three of us, the baby should have a spectacular life."

"The baby," I say, starting to get the big news now, feeling it unfold in me like I've swallowed an umbrella.

"Because you wonder," she goes on, really reaching for my hand, practically wagging it at me. "Of course you wonder—you know this—*perfectly normal*—you wonder if you have what it takes to raise a child. If you can protect her from everything and also give her every advantage."

I have to take a deep breath as I feel my meds fall away. The pain arrives through my back, way at the lower end, and spreads like cattle prods to my shoulders and through my legs. I pull my hand back from hers to wedge it under my buttocks, trying to lift some flesh away from twisted nerves.

"Perfectly understandable you weren't up for the challenge," Marleen is telling me. "We felt the same. Until we got to know to Sylvie."

"Oh, I know Sylvie," I say out loud without really meaning to. But I do know her well, her yelling, her silence, her suspicions, her accusations. I know her persistence and her practicality, and I think I know now just how serious she was. I know now, too, how she connected with Maggie, probably thinking about parenting beyond dimensions I understood. It's not like she was hiding it: but everything she used to yell at me about, she's getting now with the women across the street.

"She's a very special person. Sylvie does everything with such intention. Very deliberate. Very thoughtful." She stops herself short, holds a hand up. "But you know all this. Of course. Better than I do."

She stops again, trying to gauge my reaction, but mostly looking like she wishes she'd kept a grip on my hand.

She takes a breath and sits herself straight. "This is news to you, isn't it?" She doesn't wait for an answer. "I didn't know…We should've talked first…I just found myself over here…"

I'm starting to come around, as the pain comes into focus and settles behind my forehead, as I start to wade through many, many questions, like how their paths ever crossed, how much and what exactly Sylvie has told them about us, if they're adopting or if Sylvie might be the one to carry it, if they know about Sylvie's bon vivant vocation, and lastly, if they plan on staying put to raise their child around here. But first I smile and wave her off, trying to convince her it's nothing. "Just a headache coming on. You have to believe me: I'm really happy for you."

"I'm so sorry," she says, clearly not buying it, "and just to be clear, we don't know how this will work. We don't know the specifics. But we've watched friends deal with standard arrangements. The three of us all grew up in standard arrangements. Standard arrangements are fine and well. But we don't think it's enough for the days ahead."

"Makes sense, makes sense…" I rub at my eyes, trying to push the ache anywhere. "I look forward to watching how everything goes."

I wave in the general direction of her window. She pushes herself up from the chair and looks where I'm pointing. She can see my clear sightlines, then looks back at me. "Gross," she says. "I hope you're not doing that."

I shake my head, yawning, still rubbing at my eyes. "A messed-up kid used to hang out in your window. Did Sylvie tell you about him?"

Marleen takes a step back, not so convinced again, reeling at the idea that I've been sitting here watching them. "No, she didn't," she says, and pulls her poncho around her. Then she marches to the kitchen to pick up her Tupperware. "This was fun," she says, shaking her head at me. "Obviously, I made all kinds of mistakes today."

"No, no…" I tell her. But I get up too quickly, my knee brings me back down, and I'm stuck in my chair as she makes her way out, I have to sit here and watch her rush from my building to hers. She stops in the middle, looks around, and flips me off, her poncho billowing around her.

I look at the empty soup bowl left in front of me. I've slurped up every noodle and crunched through every veggie. I try to think of what I missed while my face was steamed and buried, any crossed wires and mixed messages, the idea of Sylvie coming back here with a stroller.

I ping St. Louis—always thoughtful, always grounded, he knows what's what, and what's best for me. That's what I need now, someone I can count on. Someone familiar. St. Louis always knows what to say. "What was it Bram told me? Something about the next level?"

He's right there too, quick with his answer. "*A thin crust of lies and cheerful deceit scaffolded over a panorama of hatred and fear.*"

That's not it. I need to get him up to speed—and I'm grateful for it too, the pivot, the explaining, the welcome change of subject, getting some distance from Marleen and her news. "I haven't told you yet: Bram called yesterday. He actually called, and he was the opposite of his videos. He sounded totally different. Like some sort of personal self-help guru."

"He called you…a day ago?" St. Louis isn't following. I didn't give enough details, and he's distracted that I didn't call and tell him right away. I can hear his frustration, but the scope of the chaos is also tough to explain.

"He said he's been watching us, and he can see what we need next. 'Your trajectory is obvious.' That's what he said."

"We don't really do self-help stuff…" he tells me, skeptical now in addition to confused. "I don't get it. What exactly was he offering?"

I'm not exactly sure either, and I'm not so comfortable with what I heard. Motivational mumbo-jumbo about trajectories and next levels has never appealed to me. I think of bootstraps and struggles and overcoming tough hurdles—the kind of help the kid across the street would need. We're doing all right here. We have our puppy calendars. We win small awards. We've been growing steadily, and we're not especially desperate—even if I'm feeling pathetic and hobbled and less mobile than usual. Talking to St. Louis puts the right frame on things.

"Right," I tell him. "What *is* he offering? I mean, besides the book. I guess that's what I need him to explain."

"Everything. I want everything," Beau Bram tells me. He's the next call I make, after cleaning myself up, skipping a dose of pills, and flattening my hair with the palm of my hand. "So glad you've asked," he goes on. "Because I want everything, everything you've built."

I nod and stay serious, as if I'm on him word for word, weighing the proposition, measuring it carefully, and I hope he's not seeing me darting off constantly, obsessing over my reflection, giving everything I've got just to sit up straight. I apologize for the mayhem during his first call, and for cutting him off. I also take another stab at pushing down my hair.

"A lot of people are impressed," he tells me on video, and right off, it's like talking to his author photo, the esteemed gentleman-author coming alive on my screen. He's picking up where we left off: "You've got a good thing going. Lots of people think so. But you're lacking a broader reach. You should have a bigger platform, reaching more people. You don't seem to be achieving as much as you should."

Whether it's the meds or the mayhem or just flattery from Beau Bram, I can't say exactly why, but my eyes go red, and I start choking up. I can't find my breath, and my nose starts to run. My dodgy composure starts slipping fast.

"I should probably hand you off to my partner," I tell him. That's probably for the best now. "Our man in St. Louis. A very thoughtful and wise editor."

Beau Bram has been nodding, signaling that he's being patient, but now he shakes his head, like he's heard enough. He looks pinched and irritated, not so handsome at all and, suddenly, has somewhere better to be. He cuts me short and leans in close to his camera. "Let's stay on topic. Let's look at what's holding you back. Call me back when you've fired St. Louis."

It's very intense. The screen going blank. Suddenly, I feel very left alone. Like I've raced to the edge of a jagged sea cliff and a perfectly sculpted high-dive performer is charging straight past me, stretching into the dark in flawless swan form. It's an ultimatum moment, an impossible all-or-nothing too-good-to-be-true offer—and also the kind of jump I never asked for. Out of the blue, unexpected—*uninvited,* mostly—while the shape of it is still foggy: I still don't know why Beau Bram is doing this, what's in it for him, and I'm especially not sure what's in it for me, what *the next level* would be. Today on the screen he wasn't full of the rage, he wasn't the crazy man from his videos. There was no talk of lies scaffolded over anything. Beau Bram just stopped his feed. He said what he had to say then cut me off clean.

Outside, the streets are quiet, no one trudging up or racing down. Then a small explosion goes off across the street, rumbling the windows, gray smoke faintly rising, followed by a much larger, giant boom down the hill, one that makes my floor, my desk, and my screen shake.

CHAPTER TEN

ON THE SIDEWALK THIS morning, the angry woman from the library basement is holding a quiet rally. Like-minded locals, a coalition of the concerned, stand close on the corner. She steps off from the group, scanning the hillside, her layered knits close around her ankles, wisps of silver hair flowing like a storybook oracle who isn't above grudges or unfounded aspersions.

The folks she's gathered are middle aged and beyond, a half dozen with free time in the middle of the week. It's not a scrappy group, decked out in angular eyewear and carefully cinched waistlines, but each of them holds a can of spray paint. A vigilante graffiti squad who can easily pay the fines and maybe even do the time, as long it's deferred to community service. The old woman at the center keeps the focus at street level, pointing in a circle. I lean close to the window to see how this will go.

In the basement where we first met, we were both there for the poverty presentation by the academic from Afghanistan with an international watch group. Dr. Aliah Alam was the speaker who scolded us, a venerated authority who travels the globe under UN credentials leading conferences and seminars on the food and water we waste. Alam could've come and gone without much notice, lost in the flow of crusaders and advocates appearing regularly in the basements of libraries. The city excels at trauma programming like this, where the lights are dimmed and a sound system squeals before rugged photographers project war zone children onto deeply creased and retractable screens. Or novelists in safari gear read eye-witness accounts of the first thirty minutes in a South Pacific tsunami. Now and then, it's as simple as pie charts on easels, like Dr. Alam's, where the overheads are kept bright and a dozen empty chairs outnumber the antsy few on the edge of their seats. It's theatrical and immersive and gratifyingly dutiful, and Dr. Alam was part of a larger cavalcade representing the latest arenas of despair, in a room that could be reliably outfitted with a decent cookie buffet. What set Alam apart was an interview and a photo taken not far from here. In a long Afghani dress and a scarf wrapped around her head, she posed with a full scowl in front of a local homeless camp, a longstanding union of oversized tarps, the kind that usually stretch over charred beams on a house that's recently gone up in flames, as well as shopping carts and multicolored tents, all situated under a freeway overpass. It's not far from here. Just over the hill. Her arms were crossed, and she stared into the camera. A few pull quotes went viral: "unimaginable disregard," "Third World conditions, among the worst I've seen anywhere," "a humanitarian crisis and an international disgrace."

Hackles went up, city officials spoke out, and she extended her stay as a professional courtesy. Our library arranged to host a Q&A, but there wasn't time to build a crowd, so the room was littered with empty chairs. Dr. Alam sat with the reporter from her viral interview and calmly repeated her answers from before. Now dressed in the pantsuit of a European high official, she diplomatically drew informed comparisons between the urban slums of central and south Asia and the bejeweled streets of San Francisco.

We knew what she'd say, but the shock was still audible. The room turned cold, I watched us hold our breath together, and I felt the disgust and collective humiliation as we avoided making eye contact with one another. Dr. Alam spoke without apology, statistics in hand, framing the conditions in familiar contexts—refugee camps, human traffickers, gruesome battlefronts—studiously explaining how millions are forced to live and only raising her voice at our fair city's "shocking world-class lack of humanity." The hour-long dressing down was forthright and plain as day, and it ended with a humbled round of applause. The basement emptied out in a slow heavy shuffle and Dr. Alam caught the next flight to Singapore.

It was easy for the angry old woman to spot me across the room, eyeing me while Dr. Alam spoke. She pressed past the others, marching directly toward me, and when she got close, her thick lenses worked like frontline obstructers, like see-through anti-riot gear, making it clear just how close we'd be getting and keeping me from saying very much. She mistook me for a newcomer, part of the turning tide, the invisible hand that was squeezing out locals, aggravating Dr. Alam and requiring things like new transit hubs.

This morning, she's produced a piece of paper, creased and folded, which must list several target addresses. She holds it in front of her like a shaky divining rod, and while I watch from above, she leads her followers to the building across the street. She points to the sidewalk, and a man in leather shoes bends over with his paint can, hopping back to avoid spotting his pant leg. He works fast, and the others clap politely. When the group moves on, headed down the block, following the woman's list, I can read their tag from my windows: #notwelcome in a green that's neon and bright.

It's written so it's legible from my windows across the street, but it's also the first thing anyone will see coming and going from their new custom front gate.

My screen sends an alert. There's a new message from St. Louis, delivering his notes on Bram's book. He loves the story, the conflict, the London atmospherics, and Christian and Danny's ruined relationship. He is thrilled through the roof. If he had one complaint, it's maybe too on the nose. It's so timely it feels trendy. Like a TV procedural, ripped from the headlines. It's a very big stretch for us, a major departure from the hidden lives of spleens and the wonders of ocean buildings. If it were written by anyone else, by an author with less star power who doesn't command stages in English manor gardens, Bram's book would be a pass. Or so St. Louis tells me today.

He calls me early. He's anxious to go over it, ready to talk timing and promotional plans. He says nothing about Christian and his neighbor hiding from him, refusing to answer in the middle of the night. This morning, for me, that's top of mind. I just witnessed my neighbors leave fresh green graffiti.

"It's all yours," St. Louis tells me now. "You take the lead. Bram reached out to you; you should keep the ball rolling. You can work with him on next steps. I'll ramp up with Kate and start the legwork."

"Okay…" I say, but I can't find my next words. We've worked together for years, St. Louis and I, talking and checking in several times every day. Through the screen, he just helped me get past Marleen's visit, and I've watched him settle and find his legs in Missouri. The setting seems to suit him. His ideas, his beliefs, have only deepened. The kind of place where good people make good things happen.

If we could pull off publishing Bram, something like we've never done before, the windfall could be huge—and our work would change direction. Our trajectory would shift. We'd be on a fresh course, an idea that seems to genuinely please St. Louis. I can see it by the way he's glowing on my screen.

He found me a dozen years ago, when he replied to my job posting. The bank account was still shaky, I wasn't sure I could afford him. But the next step was a heavy lift, building a solid program, making our mark with the exceptionally overlooked. A partner like St. Louis, someone serious and grounded, would be a very good first step.

St. Louis was a refugee from San Francisco. He used to live across town, in a neighborhood different from mine, but he saw things how things were going, how the city was changing. He was also a public school teacher who lost his apartment and couldn't afford the jacked-up rents. He followed a girlfriend to Missouri and got into the local school system. When I posted a job announcement, he was the first to get in touch.

Articulate, compassionate, erudite, hard-working. A remarkable human being and honorable colleague. After college, he spent four years in the Peace Corps in Uruguay. After that, he considered a Franciscan seminary but sidestepped to primary school teaching.

"We're not saving lives here," I cautioned him in our first talk. "It's a long way from church work. And it's going to be thankless, especially starting from scratch."

St. Louis nodded. He said he understood. "The spirit grows through ideas—"

"Sure." I cut him off. "It's great to hear you talk like that. Just really great. But I also have no clue if this will work. You might be looking for another job a year from now."

"I have all the confidence…" And he went on from there, an over-zealous applicant dismissing the actual labor and getting lofty about humankind and what we're capable of, the splendid and unique, transcending the ordinary, showing readers paths beyond everyday limits. That was how he saw our venture together—bigger than politics, deeper than entertainment—all of which so far has dramatically culminated in award buzz for an up-close look at the spleen.

He doesn't talk like he used to—he's learned to pace himself. But I know where his head is, gushing over Bram's story. He's convinced it will only lead to good things. Growth, expansion, that cherished *next level,* even though we've never talked like that before. Influence and impact are things we've never measured; we've never believed there was much to bother over. We're in it for the work. Just proud of our output. We've been in our groove, which has kept us to our standards, and apart from the annual dealings with puppies, we've never had to think much past that.

Sylvie used to hear us, me and St. Louis, and she'd roll her eyes and get off to work as fast as she could.

"Seems real iffy," she'd tell me. She was impressed by none of it. "This whole thing you're doing feels like a colossal waste."

"Wow…" I told her as the front door slammed. I couldn't say what upset her so much. We'd agreed things were changing too fast and too easily. The city was swelling, the streets were always clogging, and the skyline was getting pushed in alarming ways. Everything felt busier and infinitely more crowded, like there was more of everything crammed into the same space, but also like most of it was more of the same. More spic-and-span restaurants, more handwoven hygge, more glass walls and living walls and walls with tasteful retro supergraphics. More buildings like ours were getting slick makeovers, and more new ones looked very much the same, with squared protrusions trying to mimic our bay windows but with less breakable glass and special privacy tints. More limited-run cars took up limited street parking, brazenly daring more glass breakage too. More office workers on the sidewalk carried more pricey tote bags stamped with messages proclaiming more is always too much. Resistance had its own brand, its own signs of anti-consumption. I watched Sylvie try to dress down, try to look inconspicuous, hyper-careful about her choices, her shoes and her watches, her bags and her scarves, convinced that understatement wasn't a statement, too.

I thought of my work as a quiet sort of remedy, a growing stack of paperbacks that marked substantive alternatives—the standards that St. Louis cared so much about. I managed a workaround, a setup that protected me and allowed me to watch the rest through windows that were easy enough to replace. But now Sylvie was in it, one of the many walking downhill and back up again at a pace I've never experienced myself. We shared gunfire and sirens. She accused me of secrets and unspoken agendas, we yelled and shouted and tore into each other before she finally left. Seven years later, she's come back to more changes, maybe finally catching up with them, finding what she needs right across the street.

I don't think she's ever read one of our books. Ultimately, she found my world unworthy, convinced she could find better somewhere else. When she resurfaced a couple days ago, it felt like a courtesy, an obligatory drive-by. Like an envoy or an emissary from a strange land not so far away, who meant no harm but also did me little good. Her second visit, post-mugging, was a throwback to old times, proof that we were no good at taking care of each other.

St. Louis starts up now, charging ahead of me. "We should definitely build on Beau Bram. Get Kate in the loop ASAP. Spread the word fast, approach others at the same level, and talk about how we can leverage this. We should use this as a chance to ramp up and grow."

"Okay…" I say again.

"Okay…" he says back to me. His voice turns curious. "Why do I sense something's up? You still don't look well."

I'm still looking ugly, my neck and my shoulders still stressed, especially since skipping my pills again today. But I have to get through this. I need to explain what I've decided: I'll give him the reins and keep Beau Bram out of it. I'll funnel the puppy funds direct to St. Louis. He can do what he needs to do. Build an empire. Take the world on. I see now that I've been holding him back.

I look at the screen, where St. Louis drinks coffee, waiting for me to explain myself. He wipes his mouth on his sleeve, but I can't see much behind him. He always keeps the door closed. His wife never pops in. In the rooms beyond the door, there's either nonstop bliss or painful, messy havoc, neither of which he's ever shared with me. We sit like this often, several times during the day, the video link streaming while we look at things together, passages, titles, changes we'd like to see. Long, quiet stretches while one waits for the other, easier than making more calls through the day. He's typing something now, working on a different window, pausing to smile when he notices me watching. I have no idea how my decision will affect him. Not really, not personally, beyond the face I look at every day. Maybe he's been professional, keeping boundaries between us—which would make us lopsided, I've been leaning on him but he's never leaned back. My rock, my partner—he doesn't see me that way. He doesn't think of me like that, maybe because he doesn't want to hear it, or maybe worse, he's seen too much that's ugly, he doesn't appreciate the choices I've made.

"What's up?" he says now. "I can tell something's bothering you."

It's a good time for a pill. A good time to get foggy, get some distance from the pain, just to get through this.

"Shouldn't I bring Kate in?" he's telling me now. "I think she'll have a lot to say to Beau Bram"

Our arrangement has worked well, and I'll leave it to them, St. Louis with Kate, to figure things out. Kate will probably have a fit when she hears what's happened, left behind with St. Louis to miss out on Bram. I can't imagine she'll be her default joyous self. But I can't let her near him. I don't know what she'd say to him, or what newfangled universe she's invented now. St. Louis has shared her latest: her new belief in flat animals, extending the phenomenon. Another why-not theory just waiting for evidence of flat owls and flat bobcats, flat cobras in flat India and flat whales in the depths of the flat China Sea. At the same time, her work has hit new levels. Kate can take credit for the spleen book on any shortlist. I can't deprive St.

Louis of the special sauce that she's got. I'm still watching him work now: they're an enviable team.

I probably missed something there. Cut myself short. For a minute, there was something between Kate and me, something that I could've pursued, something that was completely out of step for me. It would've been stupidly arrogant, the boss trying to seduce his vibrant coworker. And what would happen next anyway? I could've moved to New York, seen where things went, offered my thoughts on tigers and the cosmos, and watched how they stacked up against pro-hockey charisma.

We'd get an apartment in Brooklyn; I'd hole up there, and Kate would leave every morning to navigate streets I don't know at all. It's hard to imagine, but if I'd persevered and won her over, convinced her of my thinking, spent every day digging up stories and pictures, evidence that our world is pretty remarkable as is—the lives of the spleens hidden in our own bellies and the towers underwater that will be our salvation—but if I did spend the rest of my days on that project, wooing a dazzling partner with the exceptionally overlooked, would that be enough? Could I hold her attention? More than the thrill of whirlwind crackpots, theories whose appeal is that they can't be proven? Maybe the half-baked is Kate's big advantage, what keeps her ticking, an ache for something she can't hold or have. That sounds a lot like being with Sylvie, our plan for a child she always kept at arm's length. Our future was nearly as distant and sketchy. It's a lonely place to wake up every day. At the end of it, look how brightly Kate's universe shines, how widely, eagerly her work is celebrated. Then consider how small mine has been. I know my preference, and I know what she'd give up. This is what's best for her—and St. Louis—and probably what I owe them.

This morning, this decision, it's a move against romance, a turn away from the big splash and a swan dive over a blind cliff's edge.

My new workaround, the best solution I can engineer: I'll work with Bram myself, without the talents of my partners, so the risk is all mine. If his book isn't the masterpiece St. Louis thinks it is—if that passing weak spot, that lack of empathy in London neighbors, sinks the whole book—the ship will go down with only me in it.

"We have to shake things up," I tell St. Louis, and when I talk through the rest, he doesn't seem to follow. I watch him nod, half-listening, glancing now and then, and I can tell he's working on another open window. Probably making more notes on Bram's London story. Maybe hoping I'm not sharing something too personal. "My plan is to give you whatever you need. That's what needs to happen here. I can see what you want now. You and Kate will be better off."

"Um…" he says, finally turning toward me. "That doesn't make sense. Where'd you get that idea?" I have his full attention now, looking straight at me through our screens' feed.

I scratch at my knee. I part my hair down the middle. A little sawdust falls from the floor above. "Things aren't so good here," I tell St. Louis. "And I'm thinking they haven't been good for a while. It's time for a change."

"A change?" he says back to me, and he starts looking irritated. "I have no idea what you're talking about."

"Over and out," I say and cut the video. I don't intend to be harsh. He must've heard my voice tremble, saw my eyes start to tear up. In the moment, it felt like something Bram would do. Another moment later, it doesn't feel good at all. The last thing I see is St. Louis waving, trying to flag me, incredulous at watching me shut things down.

I try to catch my breath, glad I skipped the medication. I wipe at my eyes, breathe through the next moment, and look down at my knee distended in new, grotesque ways. Across the desk, the windows rattle ever so slightly—a small breeze passing, but they're loosened by the explosions that come every day now. When I look outside, a bad mood persists; irritability has become general. Blue tarps mark the most recent house fires. On the sidewalk below, neon-green writing spells it out for me, a panorama of fear right there in plain view.

CHAPTER ELEVEN

CANNES, DAVOS, BASEL, MIAMI, Mexico City, Havana, Los Angeles, and Beijing. This is Bram's itinerary for the next few months, at least as I can piece it together. He has a job, an endowed chair, vaguely tethered to a state university. But it doesn't slow him down much. He speaks at festivals and conferences, booked almost nonstop, with little visible fallout from recent outbursts. I'm not exactly sure how he and I will work together, how we'll get anything done. I've tried calling twice today, but I haven't heard back.

I've spent most of the day refusing calls from St. Louis. We have a lot of projects going, the small spleen book among them, and there are agents, editors, vendors, and suppliers I have been working with exclusively—all loose ends he'll have to pick up and pull together. There are files, account numbers, and contacts to share. This breakup won't be clean. But I try not to worry over his new workload. Big changes can be messy in all kinds of ways.

My knee throbs again, and I consider a pain pill. But I need my wits about me, and I'm not wearing the Velcro brace like I should. I catch myself itching through my pant leg, digging in fingernails, though I know that's no help.

I stick close to the screen, clicking past the everyday queue, hunting for a new message from Bram. I refresh and refresh, and the day starts getting long with the knowledge that Bram hasn't signed any papers yet. There's no agreement between us; apart from our brief calls, I have no formal assurance. We also haven't talked money— I'm horrified by the figures bouncing through my head. *Everything. I want everything.* That's all I'm going on. Flattery and vague promises. That's all it takes, that's all I need to abandon my world, the work I've built my life around, the colossal waste of time that's brought me to this point.

Outside, the graffiti has withstood its first cleaning. The sidewalk around it is wet and damp, like someone tried scrubbing it off overnight. But it's still bright neon, still hostile and seething. When I look down, I can see the damage I've done using a pen to scratch around my kneecap, digging into my pant leg, getting a rush through the nerves there. It's more gratifying than fingernails but definitely not smart. I have to watch my own instincts. Some inner part of me has come unglued.

I turn back to work, but I'm already stuck, lost without my team. Before today, St. Louis and Kate took care of everything. Now I'm distracted by designs, the ins and outs of promotions and how to package a book I'm still not so sure about. Right off the bat, I'm ahead of myself, worried about the cover: Big Ben, the Gherkin, a cracked treatment of Tower Bridge. Outlines of falling figures pasted on the Union Jack. Horrible ideas, far from our standards, what Kate could whip up. I'll have to hire new help, someone seasoned and available, who gets the big risk here, but it's another unknown among many. I don't know Bram's work style, how he handles his editors, how he'll treat whatever marketing I cook up. Maybe he's a diva. That's a reasonable expectation. He may believe every word he has ever written is untouchable and sacred. Or maybe the opposite: the way he's racing around, he may be inclined to leave it all up to me.

"I'm leaving it all up to you," Bram tells me, returning my call with zero formality. We've hardly said hello. He doesn't apologize for the slow reply, and he doesn't acknowledge my news about cutting ties with St. Louis. "Take a breath," he tells me. "Slow down. We can make this very workable. Send me your paperwork. I'll get it signed right away."

He can see me nodding and smiling on the screen. "Great," he says and cuts the cord fast.

The screen goes dark, and I'm left with my reflection. Haggard as ever, still ruddy in the face. I didn't have a chance to talk about anything: not my lost staff or the changes I'd like to see in the manuscript. But I guess this is it. This is how it'll be. Brief access when he's got it. He'll call when he can. I got only the shortest glimpse—I couldn't tell where he was calling from. It looked like a hotel room, somewhere nicely furnished where the sun has already set.

I loosen the Velcro, I double-check the green graffiti, and after a deep breath, I click on the queue for what I've missed today: A CEO's treatise on social contributions. An elegiac biography to a fallen nineties rock star. A parody set in Kazakhstan, where a bureaucrat tries to introduce a modern alphabet. A novel set during a California mudslide. Another about a love affair with a home digital assistant.

I shouldn't be looking. I need to shut down my access. I won't be so connected, not in the same way, but it's a habit I'll have to break. On the screen, my reflection is shocking. The red lines on my cheeks and chin have gotten thicker, blood vessels bursting, screaming for attention.

"Can we talk?" St. Louis titles his next note. "Are you serious? Is this happening?" He's been sending messages like that all day.

I go back to Bram's manuscript, skimming and scrolling until the tone-deaf moment, when a Londoner doesn't answer his neighbor's call. It's sort of a long passage. I end up highlighting most of it, mak-

ing a big bright yellow block, and beside it, I write a note, my one
critique: "Are you sure this is what you want? Is this what we want to
reflect back to the world?"

I want to know Beau Bram's honest opinion, pointing him to
page seventy-two. I bundle it with an amended boilerplate contract,
lifting out my old company and replacing it with just my name,
first and last. And then I start to feel better. I sit myself upright, as
much as I can. Things are moving in new directions. I am ready to be
delighted. It's still totally unclear what Bram has in mind, but now
I know what that's like, what everyone else has been through: what
Sylvie felt like when she walked out our door, what St. Louis did
when he jumped to Missouri, what the kid across the street must've
been thinking driving away in a shiny Range Rover. None of us have
the same invisible hand pushing. But all of us have one. Mine re-
plies quickly with the scene rewritten, a flawless few paragraphs that
don't impact the rest. No changes are needed to incorporate Bram's
revision. A surgical addition that takes care of my concerns, at least
regarding the book's content.

"I'm not sure I agree, but if this is what you need…" Bram adds
a note in response to mine. "Do you really think most people answer
their door in the middle of night? Wouldn't most people think twice?
You live in a city, you know how things get. I think it's universal—
you'd wait for it stop, then roll over and get back to your dreamtime.
You gotta have thick skin in places like London—or LA or New
York. Wherever. You have to look the other way quite a bit. All the
time. Otherwise, you go crazy. To live together, to get along side by
side, we have to hold onto a reasonable level of distrust."

But he's happy to oblige with his polished revision, allowing the
London neighbors to answer their door. It gives Christian a chance
to interact, to have his call heard, to move forward with some faith
that those closest have his back—even though, by the end, they prove

that they don't. At least now, with the revision, everyone has a shot, an opportunity to act like I think they should.

I'm crafting a cautious thank you when Marleen lets herself in. I start lifting myself up, moving to greet her without looking too perturbed, but she waves me back down, shaking her head, putting a finger to her lips, signaling she'll be quiet. She's not here to make a scene. The last time I saw her, she was flipping me off as she charged across the street. Now she's delivering warm bread wrapped in a vintage tea towel embroidered with the Golden Gate. She passes it to me carefully, solemnly, like an offering before Solomon, and then watches as the loaf does what it's supposed to do, radiating from my fingers through my arms to my shoulders. She looks pleased with herself, and in a big puffy jacket, one that plumps wide around her, she plants herself in the low-slung chair.

It's a cake-like confection with spices and nuts, a savory universe that unfolds in my mouth. I close my eyes and give myself over to it. For something like this, heating me up from the inside, Beau Bram can wait. Everything can.

"Another mental health day?" I'm asking, my mouth full, leaning back, skipping utensils, just breaking off chunks, one after the other. I realize I've been silent for a minute or so.

"I know I shouldn't be here," Marleen tells me kind of quietly. She's been patient with my gorging, slouching in her jacket and crossing her feet now stretched out in front of her. "But how are you doing?" she says and looks up at me. I have to break my bread stupor. I have to give her a look back. I have to slow my chew, and I have to wonder why she's so comfortable here.

"Getting by," I tell her. "Hanging in there," I say, trying to tone down the suspicion, and I go ahead and break off a nice healthy chunk. I don't know what she's up to. I don't want it to be anything. I just want to sit here and be at one with this feeling. This feeling that my body can still do this, it can still find some comfort, be at ease on the inside, warm and contained and away from my head. But that's all over now. That feeling has come and gone, and Marleen is still here, the engineer of my swooning, and aside from the graffiti, none of the bad stuff has changed between us.

"You still look like hell," she tells me. "That's obvious from across the street."

I leave the bread on my lap long enough to smooth my hair.

"How's it going there?" she asks and points at my knee.

The Velcro straps hang off the sides of the brace, and my pant leg, an already-worn pair of green slacks, has given way to a small pen-sized hole. It's about to expand to a wide, full-sized rip.

"It gets itchy," I tell her. "Can't really help it."

"So let's get right in there…" she says and leans forward, reaching for the stiff plastic brace. I start to swivel away, cradling the loaf still warming my thighs, but she stops me with both hands. "Hold on now," she says, and works quickly to set the brace on the floor, then sticks a finger through the pant's hole. In a single invasive movement, she rips it open, pushing the lower half down to my sock.

"Much better," she says, settling back in her chair, and there it is in bright daylight, grossly swollen, with new striations from my scratching, like a discolored and plumped-out cauliflower. The pen marks haven't helped, aggravating the bulge and nudging the inflammation. It's hard to look away because it's looking back at me, or it seems to be anyway: at just the right angle, I can press and squeeze the scratches and lumps until they mash together and look like an old face, with a scratch for a frown and creases for pinched eyes and blotchy skin like any weathered old man. This one is aggravated, feverish, and tired—cringing in annoyance, like I've left him down there and he knows I've done him wrong. The skin there is hot, and when I stop poking at it, the geezer expression melts away too.

"Your pills aren't working. Obviously," Marleen tells me, shaking her head and sliding back into her seat. "You need to switch up your regimen. Be aware of the pain and what you're experiencing." She takes a deep breath and exhales dramatically, arms swooping in demonstration, then I watch her get comfortable all over again.

I secure the bread one more time and reach for the fallen pant leg. It doesn't stay up, falling back to my ankle, so I have to just sit here and be exposed. The wrinkled face I saw before is now a denture-less crank, slack and exhausted, like he's trying to sleep, aching to get comfortable. I have to poke at it again to make it go away.

"You shouldn't be working." She crosses her ankles again. "That's pretty obvious, too. No driving heavy equipment or big decision-making."

I tear at the bread and take another mouthful. I've made a big dent. The tea towel is full of crumbs, and though I regret nothing, I probably shouldn't eat more until Marleen has left. Just one more chunk and then another before I have to see my neighbor shaking her head.

"You're a mess," she says. "You know that, right?" She gets up in a resigned way, hands deep in her puffy jacket, shoulders high around her head, but then she points me toward the bed, away from my desk, like a benevolent dictator swaddled in high-performance down who won't take no for an answer. "Get some sleep. Let your body heal. Spend the day with no screens."

"Yes. Of course. You're right," I tell her with my mouth full all over again. After setting the loaf aside and brushing away crumbs, I hop across the room in an exaggerated way, sitting myself down on unmade sheets and covers. She nods, then spins back to the door. "No heavy equipment," I call after her between chews, though I don't really mean it, just hoping to appease her, get this awkwardness over and be left alone with what's left of the bread.

"You'll be back on the dance floor before you know it," she tells me, and on her way, she does a little pirouette, one hand over her head, her puffy jacket floating up from the floor. She closes the door behind her, and I manage a big swallow, tracing the warmness as it goes.

But I can't really explain it, what exactly just happened, why Marleen showed up here. And when can I get more wonder-bread in my mouth? I wonder, too, what Sylvie signed up for, getting involved with these women. Are we allies now, united against our neighbors and their green graffiti gang? But most importantly, why is the loaf suddenly so far across the room?

My head hits the pillow without really meaning to, and there doesn't seem to be much I can do. My knee wants to call it quits: when I nudge it now, it turns a deeper bruising red, like I've poked the old man square in the cheek, but it's still not enough to knock him awake. My leg doesn't budge. It's happy horizontal. And I'm feeling so full with my stomach stretched out, it's as if the loaf wants me this way. I could just stay here, let my eyelids get heavy, feel my breathing get deeper. But even as I doze off, I know this feeling. Like I'm not where I aimed to be but everyone else has different ideas. It's been this way since forever, since my Capezio period, that stormy day on top of that arch in St. Louis. When I reported what happened, when I told my missing chaperones, they sent me home right away, before I could compete. I was escorted off quickly, made a whirlwind departure and never quite got it, why I had to be punished and couldn't participate. It felt undeserved, like I knew better for myself, better than anyone else.

Years later, I searched public records for molesters in the region and found one of similar height active in that same period who specialized in bad weather at major monuments. A local detective worked with a heroic mother and made clever sense of the predator's patterns. A newspaper report read like a suspense novel, piecing together a penchant for boys and memorials. The story makes sense. I can see now what I couldn't then. I can pinpoint that definitively, I can name his intentions justly, and I can claim for myself a close call with true horror. I can say the threat was real, and I was sent home for good reason. Caution was warranted. My chaperones were protecting me. And I take comfort now in knowing that stranger was prosecuted. Still, for myself, the threat remains vague, and most of my memory isn't about a lurking giant; it's about being whisked away. My obliviousness is the truest thing for me—and the sense that's an unavoidable way to be. There's always something missing, the full picture is usually blurry, and we should celebrate when someone puts things in clever order. The stack of my books on my desk is a tribute to that. And now my eyes start to close, also without meaning to.

I wake up hours later and surf on Bram's history, stuffing a pillow under my knee and another behind my head. From bed, I can follow him: Frankfurt, Rio, Hollywood, Bangaluru. Several years ago he did a travel series for a luxury bag brand, providing voiceovers for a dozen city guide videos. I click on San Francisco and wince at the dated recommendations. Clubby hotels that have since gone shabby, artisan bakeries that have exploded internationally, and precious ceramics stores that have long since boarded up. Vienna, Milan, and Stockholm are others, and in each, the ceramics look about the same. Bram repeats the same tagline at the end of each. "Cities are super. Let's have some fun."

It's another side of Bram I didn't know about: the globetrotting spokesman for high-end living. Here's handsome Bram sporting a sleek leather portfolio, perched at a café next to the Pompidou. And again with a tote, leaving a glass doorway at the base of the Parthenon. Another belongs in a direct-mail catalog, him swinging an expensive duffle as he strides through ancient Rome.

I plump my pillows. This is the man I've struck a deal with. A deal we haven't signed yet but I've put everything into. Maybe this is what he's offering, my obvious trajectory to globally branded living. Private jets to private islands, historic passages made mysterious, architectural wonders as lunchtime backdrops. Ridiculous. Grotesque. Leveraging his serious work for a glossy, studded paycheck.

Sponsorships, appearances, getting paid to stand in front of things. I don't know how that's time well spent. I don't know if I could leave anything important to be a spokesmodel for fine leather goods. In his shoes, my future shoes, I would stand in front of different things. Try to frame different pictures. Not sure what exactly, but off the top of my head: the miseries of forced migrations, the gut-sink of ruined reservoirs, maybe heartbreaking fields of industrial waste. Sounds trite as I think it. Like a talking-point listicle, the to-dos anxious celebrities have already ticked off.

I haven't cleaned my flat in days, and the garbage is piling up. My desk is thick with bread crumbs and sawdust, and across the floor, boxes from EggSprout are starting to leak. It's all my own trash. Those rotting lunches are mine. That pile of laundry waits for me. And yet I'm not budging. My knee stays on its pillow, and my feet aren't taking me round with the broom. It's as if we're all waiting, expecting nothing much to happen, because Beau Bram is calling the shots now.

When a knock comes, the room has gone dark, and the evening light gives a calm dusky glow. With another knock, a lot more forceful than Kenny's, I can feel my little nap hasn't been much help. I'm still groggy, my knee is still inflamed and itchy, and when I get to the door, hopping all the way, I'm wrapped again in a blanket dragged with me from the bed.

This time, it's the police, and their eyebrows go up. I try to put weight on my knee but end up doubled over. I let out a little yelp and grab for the wall.

"You okay?" one of them asks, a broad-shouldered man in storm trooper boots. "Can we come in?" he says, peering around the door as he pushes it open.

I hop back and nod, waving them past me. I try to straighten myself and find some normal breath.

"We've had complaints from this building. We've been to this address several times. We're circling back now with some questions about the man who lives upstairs."

His partner stands behind him, taking in my surroundings. The dusky light has quickly dimmed. Still draped in the blanket, I must look like a squatter who's taken over the place.

"You alone here?" he asks, but his partner shuts him down, waving him off and stepping between us.

"What about the man upstairs? Kenneth. Do you know him? Do you interact with him?"

"I do," I tell him. "I've just started to get to know him. I've enjoyed our conversations. Maybe you've read some of his thoughts online."

"What happened here?" the officer asks, pointing at my knee. I've figured out I should stand with one hand on the wall, the bad leg bent and lifted. The knee is still exposed, the ripped pant leg at my ankle. It's ugly red, not happy getting dragged around, like it's ready again to start yelling at me.

"Oh, that." I try shrugging. "An accident. The front stairs. I wasn't watching my step."

"You've had it checked out? You've been to a doctor?"

"An ambulance. The whole works. Kenny was very helpful."

"Kenny? Kenneth upstairs?" The officers look at each other. "He was involved in this?"

But I have to catch my breath. Keeping it lifted is not good, so I slump as fast as I can to the chair. "Just a minute," I tell them and drop into the low one. I explain what happened, avoiding implications. I'm very deliberate and clear that it was an accident. I add that Kenny has been by to check on me. He even offered to help clean things up.

The officers nod. They each have their own notebook, which they show to each other, nodding at each other's notes.

"What do you know about the explosions across the street?" the first officer asks.

"Excuse me?" I say, not expecting that one. "What explosions?"

"You haven't heard explosions from the remodeled property? We've had several complaints. We're trying to confirm them."

"I'll confirm them. I'll confirm them." And suddenly, I'm surprised someone else has called them in. Suddenly, I'm not sure why I never have. I feel negligent and complicit. Not half the good neighbor I think I am.

"Next time, call us, would you?" the second officer says. "About any of this stuff."

I apologize and agree, and I try to be gracious. I get up to see them out, but they both wave me down, insisting I stay off of my feet. Once they're gone, I lift myself and get up just enough to see them crossing, headed for Max and Marleen's building, careful to step over the #notwelcome graffiti.

It's quiet and getting darker. I fall back in the chair. I fall asleep there and wake up deep in the night, hours before morning. Out the window, the skyline is having a field day shimmering and twinkling, dressed up in its city best.

CHAPTER TWELVE

MY SLEEP PATTERNS ARE off. I've already checked for word from Bram, and I've watched the sun come up against the fog hanging tight.

I'm at the top of the stairs, outside my front door, watching Lennon struggle with my deliveries. His thick legs look heavy in his snug EggSprout shorts, and under his EggSprout hat I can see he's short. I don't really need a new delivery, but it's a standing order I don't want to mess up.

"Have you always been an EggSprout?" I ask him this morning. "What did you do before you drove that van?"

"Law school," he tells me, wiping his forehead, and he points at my knee. I'm still in the slacks with one ripped pant leg, so he can see what I'm dealing with. But the swelling has shifted to a friendly pink shade. "Summa cum laude," he adds, looking up at me. "Headed for intellectual property. Graduated, passed the bar, and then ran out of gas." But even this doesn't fade the glow in his cheek, the sparkle in his eye, all of him rosier than he has a reasonable right to be.

I open the top box as he holds the stack of them. I find a pudding cup, then a second in another. I motion for him to sit and join me, and he puts the delivery down in the vestibule behind me.

"How'd you do it? How'd you quit?" I find two of EggsSprout's biodegradable spoons and pass one to him. We sit down together and scoop through tapioca served in sensible portions.

He wipes his mouth on his sleeve. "By the end of law school, I didn't even know how miserable I was. When I figured it out, the damage was done. I was overeating to cope and I couldn't even see how big I was getting." He rubs his belly in a circle and grins up at me. "This job is perfect." He licks his spoon dry before handing cup and spoon back grandly.

I don't know why he thinks that. It looks like hard labor, and it's full of temptation. "So you just hit a wall? You woke up one day and said, 'The law's not for me.' Three or so years of study, probably a mountain of debt, and you decide to chuck it and jump onto something else?"

Lennon takes it as a cue. He gets himself on his feet, pushing up with both hands until he's over his stump legs. He looks up at me. "No one stopped me from quitting," he tells me. "And no one's stopping me now."

He gives me a little salute off his EggSprout hat, then he hops down the stairs before he stops in the street. There he pulls down his hat, puts out his arms, and does a flawless cartwheel, before climbing in his van and speeding to his next delivery.

Inside at my desk, there's more frustration from St. Louis, along with several authors expressing concern. I'm not usually so silent. I always stay on top of things, responding to our clients as promptly as I can. To St. Louis, I send a brief note, apologizing again for the abrupt notice and offering a timeframe, suggesting we talk in three or four weeks. I figure a deadline might be helpful for us both.

The incoming queue brings an anthology of Sherpas, a tirade against childbirth, a collection of fables based on Central American juntas, and a compendium of photographs of burnt school buses collected from over sixty-four countries. I shouldn't be looking. This is a kind of torture. But I do notice the tone, how sad the queue feels today. Things seem to be centered on what's gone missing.

Most of these submissions—these meticulous creations, these pinnacles of passion—won't get read past the first lines of their descriptions. St. Louis will have less time than ever, and so there they will sit, less a pipeline of opportunity or a map of surprises than a shorthand index, a thumbnail register. It doesn't feel right, of course, just skimming the surface—but unless St. Louis ramps up like I think he will, the full manuscripts won't ever be read.

By noon, the morning feels like a full week, and I'm trying my best to stay out of bed. I want to be ready for Bram, so I'm showered and shaved. I'm also back in the ripped pants, because oxygen seems right. Fresh air must be a good thing, and I can keep the shabby tatters out of Bram's view. I can poke at it now without getting it angry. The inflammation looks larger but more uniform, puffier but less blotchy, and when I push and squeeze it, trying to find the craggy old face, there's just a thick, dull pain.

The fog has stayed low all the way through the noontime, and the office workers this morning were bundled in black and gray. Scarves and overcoats, heads down and at a solid pace. No one is walking back uphill yet. The focus so far has been on the bus routes below.

Down the hill, I've been hearing the demolition continue—not the monster explosions, but heavy equipment moving debris, bringing the panicked dings of trucks in reverse and the scrapes of heavy metal scooping along concrete.

Still no sign of Kenny. And none of Darrel. This morning when I took my pills, I thought of his insurance and disagreeable meds. I can't begin to speculate on what he's been going through, but I should. I should lean into Kenny, try harder to hear him, and I should've made an effort with Darrel. At least covered the basics, how long he's been here, what he thinks of the graffiti, what he'd like to see happen with the new transit hub. What anybody asks everybody day in, day out. But you wait long enough, people think you're not interested. People think you've moved on, that you live in your own bubble. He probably thinks I don't think about him at all.

Things will change when my knee heels, when my body's more mobile and stops looking so angry. I'll get myself out, meet Darrel for coffee, bring Marleen some EggSprout, finally see what's left from the demolition down the hill. It's been three days—or four? I'm not sure. But a few doors down, there's a tree with red bark that's about to bust open with giant white blooms. I think I might have time for things like that now.

I check my messages to make sure I haven't missed Bram. An acquaintance, an occasional reviewer, sends a disturbing one instead: "Can we talk? I'm concerned. I've heard you're taking Beau Bram's next novel. I have to be frank with you. I think it's a mistake."

Her message is straightforward, and she includes her phone number in case I don't have it. Within minutes I get a similar one from a popular novelist who's befriended us, warning pretty much the same. "Have you gotten through the manuscript? I don't think you should touch it—if it's not too late."

My stomach turns a little as a third one comes in. "If you haven't been warned yet, let me be the first. I know it's not my place. You know your own business. But I have to speak up. Read really closely. Make sure you're comfortable with what he's promoting. And do some research on Bram. It looks like he's cracking up."

"Your first instinct," he goes on, "is to be flattered. But don't get seduced by his celebrity machine. The book has some hidden eggs. Some coded subtext, which you may have missed. They went over my head on my first read. Get some second opinions. Ask me, if you want to. Just keep in mind, you weren't his first choice, many others have passed on it—that manuscript has been making the rounds—and there are plenty of other fish in the sea."

My first impulse is to pull up the document, but the next message is from Bram, who is ready to chat via video. I rub at my eyes and try to smooth my hair. I greet him in a voice that's way too chipper.

"Hello yourself," he says back to me, taking a quick assessment. "Looks like you're feeling better. Have you been sick or something? You haven't looked well the last times we've talked."

"A minor injury. It's nothing." I can feel my smile fading. "A minor assault. Nothing too bad."

"Assault?" Bram says, leaning close to his camera, trying to look around me. Out of view, below the screen, the extra inflammation feels hotter but less itchy, and I'm still thinking the ripped pants were the right way to go. "What are you doing getting assaulted? How does something like that happen? I don't think that sounds smart."

"Well, it's not smart," I tell him. "And it wasn't really an assault. I shouldn't call it that. I was trying to help a neighbor and ended up falling."

"A neighbor?" he says, looking more worried than ever.

"It was nothing. Really."

But I can see him look away now, turning a little pinched while he weighs this out. He looks up again, shaking his head. His voice even trembles. "I get it now. I understand. This is why you wanted to change that one passage. You think the world's a kinder place than it actually is—and you've broken your leg trying to convince yourself."

"Oh, now, Bram. Nothing's broken."

"Oh my god," he says back to me.

I appreciate his concern, but I'm disturbed by the assumption. He thinks I'm naïve, some sheltered idealist, a shut-in bookworm who only lives through a screen. "It was just a trip and fall. And my leg isn't so bad. You're really reading too much into it…"

"Am I?" he says as he winds himself up. He looks close to tears now, shaking his head and wiping his cheek. It's another side of Beau Bram I never thought I'd see. If he's going to lose control, I thought he'd get angry and have one of his yelling fits. But this is different. "Is there someone taking care of you? Do you have someone close by? Should I send a caretaker and set up something regular? What are you doing for food?" Bram doesn't blink while he takes a deep breath. "Oh my god. You poor thing. You can't see what's happening. What you're doing to yourself…"

I try to keep smiling, but I really don't like this, how he's thinking of me now, so fragile, so obvious, and like he must know better. Another sort of person would take one look and try to be a comfort—show some strength, some poise, some shred of basic calmness, with the idea that it rubs off, that I'd feel it too. A lot like warm soup or a hot loaf of bread. But this thing with Bram is in another direction. He only pops up with big promises, or panics and falls apart.

"Did you know I'm getting pushback?" I try to avoid looking at him. "People are telling me to take a second look. You've shopped this around? You've talked to other editors? Have you even had a chance to look at our contract?"

"What…?" he says. One last tear is dropping before he's turning a different color, paler, less pink, closer to his breakdown videos. "Of course I've talked to other people…" After a quick sniffle, he catches his breath, but his mood keeps turning, and he keeps staring at me, like he can't quite believe it, how quickly I've turned against him. "But no one takes the kind of risks you take. No one is committed the same way you are," he tells me, shaking his head again, hurt that he has to explain this to me.

"Okay, okay…" I try to back down, to sound apologetic. But I also feel like sticking up for myself. I've ditched everything for Beau Bram. I should know what I've done it for, and I ought to have some say in what happens next.

"Yes…okay…let's take a step back. Let's try to remember: this is an experiment, a joint exercise…." He's sitting up straight now and taking deep breaths. "An investigation. We will both be better, different men when we're done with this."

He makes a big gesture, dropping his finger toward the keyboard, stopping the call and sending the screen blank. The video goes dark. I've got no more real answers. Then a message from Bram delivers our signed contract, followed by four or five anxious ones from other authors, cautioning me against going further.

It's all too much. I have to catch my breath, and when I look out my window, there's just what I need, a remarkable thing to witness: a little boy skipping downhill, racing at full stride, at a hair-raising pace. He's alone in the street, in familiar-looking dance tights—dark blue Capezio for boys—and tan dance slippers. The momentum is frightening. He's almost a blur. He looks like he's close to falling on his face, twisting an ankle, probably ripping his tights and getting caught by whatever he's running from.

I can feel it in my ache, what I'm thinking deep down: "Go, boy, go." It comes from my bones, in a howl from my knee. "Get where you're going, get there fast." I push away from my desk, try to get myself down there, but I get double-crossed and end up nose-deep in delivery boxes. I reach for the brace, try to tighten the Velcro, but it's heavy and tangled. I'll go faster without it. My hideous gnarled leg is still telling me so.

At the vestibule, I consider pounding on Kenny's door. But I have to steady myself and need to focus on the stairs. Apart from pudding with Lennon, this is as far as I've ventured in several days.

By the time I'm on the sidewalk, the boy is long gone, and I'm getting the sense I've made a wrong turn. I try going back, but the maneuver is too much, and after a couple of corrective hops, I end up reeling backward into the street, scraping both elbows against the pavement.

The pain is blinding and universal, as if my full body were covered in flames. I roll onto my stomach and drag myself flat, with both legs limp behind me, aiming for the closest curb, the one with neon green graffiti. Thinking Marleen and Max might be my best hope, I guess at the buzzers on their building. I don't know their last names, and the first one I try produces a woman who says, "Buzz me again, I'll call the police." The second informs me I'm recorded on video. "Got a real clear shot, buddy," the speaker reports.

The next is Marleen, who releases the gate with a tasteful buzz. I can hear footsteps rushing down the stairs to meet me. When she gets me onto one foot, I remember she's much shorter, but she insists I lean on her. With an arm around my waist, she helps me to the top floor, step by step.

"I don't know what you're thinking," she says under her breath. She's trying not to upset me. "I thought I told you to stay in bed."

"I've made a horrible mistake. I just needed to get out." I'm about to explain more until I see where we're going, through a door that opens to a thick blanket of heat. A couple of small candles light the entry, and I can hear people laughing down the hallway. Onions and braised meats are cooking down there, as far as I can smell, and from what I can see, the walls are painted in muted earthy shades, with thick shaggy rug art hanging at different levels. The place has the feel of a big bear hug. But Marleen gently turns me, guiding me in the opposite direction, away from the aromas and conversations, toward a tidy bedroom and the edge of the bed.

"Poor thing," she says. She sits me down. She gives me a pat. She takes a step back and delivers a stern look. "What are you up to? You sure you should be out?"

She dims the room's lights and goes to pull the blinds. "Wait," I tell her. "If you don't mind, I'd like to look." I'm not getting up or going anywhere, but I lean across the bed, toward her tall windows, and try to glimpse my own home from this side of the street.

It looks abandoned and neglected. As if it weren't occupied. A stripped-down, crude space that doesn't look comfortable or even very clever. My little chair and simple table are set up at the window, like a crazy sentry, an unhinged lookout.

It's a wonder Marleen ever ventured over. Kenny must also see me as a kook, an abandoned loner who's gone off the edge surrounded by happy families and kitchen upgrades.

I lean back across the bed, stuffing pillows where they help, and watch the light dim as Marleen continues to pull down the shades. In the dimness, I see Sylvie almost ghost-like in the door to the hallway, draped in warm grays, backlit by candles, looking right at home in Marleen's apartment.

"Jesus," she says and stops at the door.

"Look what the cat dragged over," Marleen says to her.

Sylvie looks away, then to her host. "Sorry to interrupt. We were looking for rosemary..."

Marleen nods while she pulls the last blind, turning the room into a box of shadows.

"Sylvie?" I say. "Hello?" I'm genuinely shocked she hasn't said more, like she's pretending not to see me, like I'm delegated to Marleen. Even here on her friend's bed, I'm not her problem anymore.

"Hello," she finally says back, mastering a smile, then she gestures for Marleen to return and join the party. Guests are waiting. She's holding things up.

"Sleep," Marleen says to me, putting a hand on my shoulder. "You're fine here. Relax. I'm going to close the door so you're not bothered by us. Not a problem at all. I'll check back in a bit and bring some of that soup you like so much."

They close the door behind them, giggling as they go and taking the light down another notch. I try to get up once, but it doesn't go well. My head gets heavy, the shadows get deeper, and my eyes close fast once I give them a chance.

I wake up in my own bed the next morning. I'm still in my ripped pants, and when I reach for my knee, it feels smaller, less swollen and less sensitive to the touch. A depleted ice pack and heat pad are on the floor. The brace and its Velcro are tight and where they should be. The place is empty. I'm alone here, somehow.

At my desk, on the screen, a dozen messages from St. Louis and just as many from others warning about Bram. Across the street at Marleen's, the shades are still pulled and the room is dark behind them. The fog has lifted early, showing a soft, low sun.

Then I notice fresh sawdust on my sleeve and keyboard, and I can see more coming like pencil-shaving snowfall. It's been a few days, things have been quiet upstairs. But then there's a thud, another one following, like someone or something has fallen or been dropped, followed by a heavy-weighted object getting dragged across the apartment's floor. Something big is getting moved, and I can hear furniture scratching. I turn in my chair and look up at the floorboards, tracing its path from front to back, and I stop myself short of knocking on Kenny's door. I've never interrupted, through all their shouting and arguing. I've always waited for help to be requested. That's my answer to Beau Bram when he calls me thin-skinned. We have to rely on others to ask when they need it.

Out my window, a brownish rope drops and dangles. As it swings, I can see it's really an extension cord, plastic with a plug curled up on the end. In a flash it's yanked up and out of view. I lean forward and peer up, then move to a sill where I can sit and open a window, leaning out to see what's happening. Over the edge of the roof, above Kenny's windows, the beard-stubbled lady with her ample bosom swings into place, five or six feet over the edge into open air. Her gaze is directed both down and forward, directed at the sidewalk below and across the hillside, and she's rolling back and forth a little, as if trying to scooch to just the right spot. Then beside her, Devan the glazier leans out over the edge too, side by side with Darrel's masthead.

I wave up and call his name. He's flat on his stomach a dozen feet above, and he takes his time before forcing a minor smile. He's nudging the wood with his shoulder, then rolling on his side and grabbing it in a hug, extending himself so far over the edge I can see his crisp tool belt. He rolls and pulls the wooden lady to just the right spot.

The building is trimmed with slotted molding painted black, and the lady herself is painted to match Darrel's drawings, but much brighter than I expected. Her skin is light brown, her hair is platinum blonde, her lips are painted red, and her eyelids are colored green. As her body morphs into the round shape of the log, she's cloaked in a garish peacock cape that looks borrowed off of an Aztec superhero.

"She's beautiful," I yell at him and watch for an answer.

Devan stops and looks down at me, breathing heavy, not smiling. Then he gives me a quick salute. He disappears behind the roof's edge. Some hammering follows.

Her view is better, more expansive than mine.

CHAPTER THIRTEEN

LENNON RUNS FROM THE building and peels off in his van. A small crowd has gathered on the corner opposite, interrupting their commutes, missing their bus to stop and raise camera phones, recording the small fire burning on our curb.

A bonfire, not too large, sits on the edge of the gutter—a pile of papers and clothes and medical waste fueling the flames to different heights and colors. Darrel uses a ruined broomstick to tend and poke at it. The smoke is ugly, a chemical smoldering. It reaches my windows and keeps on going.

I've overslept—slept through yesterday and last night until this morning, knocked out in bed, not so interested in moving and scratching at my knee before daylight returned. The chatter from the curb seemed a little unusual, but the smell and the greenish smoke were harder to ignore. I swung my leg around and got to the windows as fast as I could.

"It all has to go," Darrel is yelling. "None of this is okay anymore." Kenny has just arrived, out of breath but stomping at the bonfire's edges. I want to head down there, I don't want this near our building, but getting to the door still doesn't go right. My muscles aren't ready for twisting. I have to reach for the desk and can at least pull my chair close enough to keep an eye on the flames. I could call the fire department, but Kenny seems to be on top of it, and I'm not sure either one of them needs the authorities right now.

It's the first time I've seen Darrel since he sped off to the hospital, bloody in the ambulance. Kenny is pushing at him and also lunging at the fire, trying to kick some of the papers to the safety of the gutter.

Darrel looks different. He's not his old self, like he's been through the ringer, through some monstrous decisions, and he's not at all happy about the results. He's gotten an extreme haircut, shaved to the skin on the front, back, and sides, except for a slim strip straddling the middle, a low Mohawk that looks both tribal and aerodynamic. He's in long shorts, not ideal for this weather, but he's also in a parka with a furry collared hood, also too much for the climate. He looks like he's maybe shirtless underneath, but he's still top-heavy, and he's moving in stiff, careful ways I can identify with.

They go back and forth, Darrel with his broomstick, Kenny with his kicking, following each other around the flames. The blaze has stopped growing, and it looks like Kenny has the upper hand, except for the thick clouds it's still sending up.

"You're crazy," Kenny is yelling. "You can't come here and do this." They both try to push the other away, and neither of them bothers with the crowd across the street. Most don't stick around, stopping long enough to record several seconds of video before running for a bus. No one intercedes. No one appears to be calling the police.

Finally, Kenny pulls the hose from the garage and turns it on Darrel's pile. He squirts at Darrel, too, who knows he's been beaten. The dousing starts a new stream of even thicker and darker clouds, and Darrel sits himself down on the wet curb, gingerly, with his back to me. Kenny spots me in the window. He shakes his head in a panicked and sorry way, then scatters the soggy embers with a punt to the street, before sprinting up the steps to apologize to me.

Darrel watches him, then looks up at my window with a cold dagger stare. But I don't think it's for me. I don't seem to register. He doesn't wave or gesture or yell. He seems more focused on the building, and, obviously, Kenny. Like before, I don't have much of a role in what's happening between them.

"I need to apologize. Again," Kenny says, stepping inside. He takes a moment to wipe the sweat from his face. "Darrel has lost it… and I know, I know, I should be checking up on you." He stops and looks around the apartment. "Look at this place. I should be bringing you stuff."

I look around. The bed and desk are still a mess, and EggSprout boxes are still piled everywhere. "I'm okay," I tell him. "I have everything I need. Perfectly capable of taking care of myself." But I hear how I sound: fed up and pissed. I get put to bed by strangers, my livelihood is in limbo, and I'm waiting for a famous stranger to somehow make it better. Darrel's chemical cloud comes through the door, and the burn in my nostrils feels just about right.

"Of course, of course…" Kenny tries to backpedal. "I should've come by to apologize. I don't know what happened. Your fall, your knee, it was probably my fault." He's looking at the brace, trying to gauge the injury.

"Just an unlucky tumble." I try to keep him at arm's length. "Just some bruises, really." And I'm relieved when I see how relieved he is, walking past me to check on Darrel from my window.

Then he sits himself down in the low-slung chair. "Darrel is back," he tells me, like the neighborhood isn't watching on high alert. But he takes a moment, looking down at his lap.

I'm relieved again that he's not over-sharing, that Darrel is demanding his attention this morning. But I can see Kenny's hurting, and I know what that's like, so I hop to my chair and give him a smile. "Tell me about it. What's going on with Darrel?"

"Darrel's not so doing well," he tells me in a lowered voice. "And I have to ask another favor."

I check the curb from the window. Darrel is bent over, calmer, but talking to himself instead of staring up at our building. It's a serious conversation. He's shaking and nodding his head. This is not the Darrel I knew before, and it's not the one Kenny has described to me, persevering through tough times and always, eventually, coming back to their love bubble.

Then I see Max and Marleen watching from their curb, in front of their building, the soles of their shoes scraping the pavement, keeping an eye on Darrel while trying to scrub off the graffiti. The fire is out, but Darrel still concerns them. His one-man conversation is getting more animated, too.

"What do you need?" I ask Kenny. "How can I help?" From my desk, I reach for a pen and start scraping at my knee in its brace.

Neither Kenny nor Darrel have gone to this extreme before. When their arguments spilled onto the sidewalk, they went toe to toe, gave as good as they got, and neither was left sitting alone out front. They always ended on the same page, arm in arm again.

But something's happened. Something pushed Darrel too far. A horror show at the hospital, start to finish. Kenny talks fast now, both of us looking down from the window.

Their arguments, he tells me, had been escalating, probably because things had gotten too stale. Too routine. Too comfortable. For reasons Kenny can't pinpoint, Darrel had started to get suspicious, a little paranoid even, making accusations in the face of so much calm. At the same time, Darrel was noticing odd illnesses. Unassigned fevers. Weird episodes with motor control. Pains in his side, numbness in his feet. Some of that probably led to the bloody accident while he was whittling on the big bearded lady.

"I encouraged him to see a doctor," Kenny explains. "I helped him find a city clinic. I told you we got stalled getting him onto my insurance." He moves to another window now, trying to get a better view. We both see Marleen and Max across the street, arms crossed, still keeping watch.

But Darrel's prognosis wasn't great. He was a medical anachronism, a "long-term non-progressor," someone with HIV who never went on a treatment because he'd never showed signs of a weakened immune system. He'd never been sick before. "That doesn't happen anymore," Kenny is quick to add. "Now, no one waits." Drugs are prescribed with the first diagnosis, and regimens begin without waiting for any illness.

"I told him it was time, and the doctors agreed. His immune system needed help." Kenny stops to look out a different window, this time at the shiny cityscape. "So we followed standard protocol, and I totally had his back. We'd take our meds together. I helped him ease into it. Most of the city is on one med or another—" He looks at me now, to make sure I'm following, and I nod like I am, like this is all common knowledge. "We talked about how normal it was, Darrel and I, and that he'd known for decades that this time would come."

Then Kenny waves out the window, unexpectedly pleasant. It's Marleen who waves back, but she looks like she won't be bringing us soup. She points to Darrel and doubles down on her scowl.

I try a little harder to be a comfort for Kenny. "Sounds like you guys were doing all you could..." But I'm barely following, and there's still no explanation for Darrel sitting down there, setting fire to his own stuff.

"Things were going okay. Until they weren't."

The standard protocol didn't work in a standard way for Darrel. It aggravated his mood and triggered his paranoia, so their arguments became more frequent, hiking up a few decibels. Of course, at the time, neither of them blamed the meds. They just thought their arguments were part of their cycle, even if they were getting more frequent.

The complications continued while things got more tense. Darrel's insides were shutting down—his kidneys, his liver, and finally his heart. All rare side effects of the standard protocol. "One in a thousand, it says on the labels." This is what Kenny reports. "Which is really not so rare. Not when you think about it. But it's not the kind of thing anyone talks about. It's right there in the fine print. 'May cause organ failure.' But I've never heard of anyone going through that."

By the time I watched him taken away in an ambulance, Darrel was suffering heart failure, and also losing his grip, racing through ugly and fast mood swings.

"And this," Kenny tells me, pointing out the window, "this is only the latest." Darrel needed a transplant, which happens every day now, but not so much without insurance, on public assistance—not a procedure that costs a cool million bucks. "Plus, he was acting crazy in the hospital. Accusing nurses, fighting doctors, attacking me. He wasn't a good candidate for the procedure. In government terms, it was good money after bad."

The thought takes my breath away. Too brutal to digest. Darrel stands up, finding a break in his own dialogue, and when he turns around with his parka unzipped and his bare chest underneath, I can see the small pump strapped to his front. It's battery-powered, and it's got its own Velcro, but it does the work his heart usually does, except it's on the outside, in a little tin box. Kenny tells me it's typically a temporary fix while patients wait for a full-on transplant. But this is it for Darrel, who's too weak and too volatile to have the kind of heart the rest of us get.

I don't know what to say. "Holy shit" is what comes out. Kenny has over-shared, and it's a heart-wrenching story, not at all what I'd planned for this morning. I feel like I should warn Kenny about the police who stopped by. But I also can't imagine adding to the drama here.

Together we turn to Darrel, who raises both middle fingers at us. His trim Mohawk amplifies his deep, dark stare, standing firm with his feet apart. His tin box is pushed forward on the center of his bare chest.

The office crowd has long since moved on. Max and Marleen have gone back inside. No one is around to capture this. But Darrel looks primed. He looks ready to attack.

And then he runs. He takes off downhill. Full speed, wide stride, with one leg limping sideways and both arms swinging everywhere. He's shouting at the top of his lungs. "Kenny!" he yells, in baritone fury.

Kenny races out the door. I watch him head down the hill. I lose sight of them while I can still hear them yelling, echoing each other's name across the hillside. I don't know how this will end, if they'll reconcile per usual and show up hips attached, back in their love bubble. I don't know if either one of them is ready for that.

Darrel's mess has left a brown muddy patch on the curb under bits of melted plastic. I'm not mobile enough to be useful or constructive. I can't skip down there and push it to the gutter. I don't know how to help—just as I never have. The last time I stepped up, an ambulance took me away. But I'm not calling the police or marking Kenny's door now. I'm not scribbling a shaming hashtag with bright indelible paint.

On my screen, I'm getting more warnings about Bram, now from bookstores and their concerned buyers, urging me to drop any plans for Bram's book.

"Maybe you've misread it," one has written overnight. "This is the worst caricature of Londoners, or anyone, I've ever read." He explains it's been circulating for a while in a samizdat, an underground circuit sharing the shocking story, a serious fumble from such an acclaimed talent.

From a bookseller in Los Angeles: "It's all there on the page, if you care to see it."

And another from Connecticut: "Bram's book," she writes, "is truly a colossal waste."

The most confounding thing is St. Louis's assessment. He voiced zero worries. Not even my concerns. He saw it as game-changer, the kind of thing that could take us to the next level, onto new trajectories.

As I scroll and click, I think about Bram's words: the book is beside the point. Together, we're headed someplace else, Bram and I are. Something TBD and yet to be spelled out. But still—if I've missed something, if the book is actually *hateful*—I should know that, too. I should have a better sense of who Bram is, what he's got up his sleeve, what he's capable of. I'd like to know who I'm giving up everything for.

When I pull up the manuscript, my perspective has shifted: Kenny and Darrel are everywhere, side by side with Christian and Danny. The London swells are still swell, just as I remember, still a well-to-do couple, still with their social circle. Bram uses some shortcuts, leaning on easy references to evoke gay London: catty chatter about celebrities, old lovers who are old friends, and meticulous attention to grooming and stylish shoes. It's not as clever as I'd thought on my first reading. Christian and Danny are a gloss on my neighbors, free from their burdens, unencumbered by their particulars. At best, Bram's men are hidden behind erudition, their mastery of political and legal details, their knowledge of decades-old culture wars. Before it turns into a hostage thriller, it is like sitting between two polished dinner guests in settings I know best from other Bram novels.

I skip ahead to Bram's sections set in outer-ring suburbs, ones full of new arrivals and the not-so-acculturated but where everyone knows the same flash points, too. This is also like sitting at a lively dinner party, another one I've never been to but based on better books by better authors.

It's all loaded with triggers. Bram is masterful at that. Any detail could get twisted around, and on this second reading, I can see how subtly he loads the arsenal that finally explodes in the last pages. But I'm still not offended. It's still a society novel. Brittle landscapes made of matchsticks meant to go up in flames quick.

Maybe he's bitten off too much—or too little. I'm still not sure. I can't really say why so many are so upset. Kenny and Darrel are worlds away. They're my first reference, more real than I can imagine, but their problems are immaterial to Danny's kidnapping and Christian's public solutions. So I have to fall back on what Beau Bram has written, and even with all the complaints in my head, it still feels effortless and seductive. I don't see why everyone is warning me off.

I've spent the afternoon re-reading. Outside, the office workers are headed back uphill, several stopping to poke at Darrel's burnt medical waste. It's a kind of El Dorado in reverse, that mythical city said to be built of gold, a treasureland constructed on top of another city. Explorers lost fortunes trying to get there. Here, it's wet trash on a worn commuter's curb.

Then I spot Kenny chasing Darrel back home, both headed toward our building, both sprinting up the stairs, the last one slamming their door shut, and the mad pounding as they climb the stairs to the rooms over my head. Across the street, Marleen and Max backed their car from their garage space, but stopped short to let the two men pass behind them. They roll up their windows and crane their necks to look for me in my window.

And in the distance, there's a brightly lit blimp cruising along the skyline, the kind rented for ball games and major corporate events. It flashes a marriage proposal and proclamations of love before turning sharp and banking out of sight.

CHAPTER FOURTEEN

BRAM IS CALLING FIRST thing, and I'm here waiting for it. All night I've been at my desk, in my chair, in front of the windows. Both legs have gone numb, and my knee looks as puffy and red as a teething baby, one that's very close to uncontrollable fits. Near midnight I started poking it again, moving the lumps around, trying to mash it into baby cheeks, with plump lips and a smashed nose, hoping to get a reaction, a comforting coo, maybe a few words of encouragement. But the lumps stayed as lumps, my injury remains a part of me, and now that Bram is calling, I'm glad it's gone numb. The sun is up, and I'm focused, almost pleasant.

When I click on the call, instead of dashing Beau Bram, there's a postcard of Acapulco pushed against his camera. Then a colorized snapshot of pre-war Berlin. When he pulls that away, I get glimpse of him shuffling papers, grinning as he does it, then putting up a beach in Vietnam, a fjord in the Arctic, a Black Sea resort, a hamam in Izmir, then a boat dock in Dakar.

"Bram?" I try to stop him.

"This is it," he tells me, and when he puts aside the photos, his cackle drops off. He points through the screen. "I'm sorry, I'm so sorry…" He's covering his mouth. "Are you still on your own? I offered some home care. What is going on? Are you getting any help?"

I know how I look. Across my face, down my neck, my blotchy, red capillaries have gotten redder and blotchier, like a subcutaneous treasure map or a sci-fi alien infection, and my posture is jacked from a night spent upright. Bram twists himself, trying to mirror it, maybe to mock it—more behavior from this man I don't really get. "I don't want to talk about it," I tell him.

"I'm sure you don't. I'm sure I wouldn't either. But listen," he says, turning a little, gathering his thoughts away from my appearance. "I'm sorry to be mysterious. I have a hundred things going."

"Well, I read your book again..." I try interrupting him. I don't want to get cut off before I get my questions in.

Bram leans close to his camera, in a rare quiet moment, then he slams on a pair of glasses, thick lenses in tortoiseshell that make his eyeballs look huge. He sniffs like he suddenly has a cold coming on. "I don't like how that sounds."

I try patting down my hair, a perpetual impulse now. Anything to make my case more convincing. "Bram—I'm sorry—but a lot of people have been warning me. It's sort of remarkable. Why is your book *hated* by *everyone*?"

"I don't know if that's fair..." He wipes at his nose, still too close and leering.

"It's totally fair." And I feel a surge of confidence. "Everybody thinks the book is pretty toxic."

"Excuse me." He interrupts me. "I've said it before: this is not about the book..." But he stops himself, bites his lip, and gets some distance from the camera. I can see him leaning back, settling into a chair too expensive for an office. "Listen. I mean. What are you doing anyway? Why are you doing this, putting little books out, trying to win little awards." He leans in close again, with his eyes even bigger. "Why are you so *small?* I mean, what's that about?"

I push away from my desk. I scratch fast across my knee. Gone are the colic cheeks of an infant. Now it's more like my knee can't breathe. Like my leg is suffocating and should get chopped off.

"It's a colossal waste of time," Bram lectures me, "what you're doing, how you're doing it. I'd think you'd be grateful I'm making time to talk..."

"Excuse me?" I say and feel my teeth clench. Out of view, under my desk, I take my leg in both hands and try pulling it away from me, thinking I'll dislodge it, disconnect it and, gripping hard enough, get it someplace else, where it's free to breathe.

But Bram has leaned back again and put his hands behind his head. He's giving me a look while he wipes his thick lenses. "Bottom line," he says, as if he's got me cornered and finally got things pegged, "what's with the damn puppies? Aren't they the real problem? What they've done to you. What they let you do. I feel like they're enabling..."

"The calendars...?"

"It's narrowed you," he goes on, and I laugh. Or I scoff, really, thinking about our frantic queue, the mess that comes at us, how much we were wading through morning after morning—a gem-sized book on the hidden wonders of the spleen doesn't come at you shouting and screaming.

But Bram charges ahead. "I mean, you're not doing your best work. You're cooped up in your place, chained to your desk. Look at you," he says, and tries again to look past me. "Did you have a flood or something? What happened in there? Looks like you live in a shaky lean-to."

I take a quick look behind me, but I know what he's seeing.

"My god," he says, his face turning red and his voice getting louder. "This is what I'm talking about. You've got to get out of there. You just...you just have to."

He's blinking fast and hard, like what he sees here is disturbing, channeling the outrage I saw in his videos. "So I'm thinking Singapore. That's a conference next week. Or Dublin, early next month."

"I can't just take off…"

"Of course you can," he snaps back. "You've got nothing going on. You've cut ties with St. Louis. You've dropped everything, *everything*, for this."

"*This*," I tell him. "I still don't know what *this* is. I didn't drop everything to go on vacation. Or to be your bag boy on a speakers' circuit." I don't know where I get it, the strength to defend myself. But he's sounding like a schoolteacher, like he can sit there and scold me. Like a chaperone sending a boy-dancer home early before he has a chance to prove himself. "Is that really all we're talking about here?"

"You're right, you're right." He throws his glasses to the side, and he studies his reflection, straightening his collar and running his hand through his hair. "I'm not explaining this well. I apologize. Really. This is a test. An experiment we're doing, you and me together. We're going to get you cleaned up, then get you turned around. Finally get you onto the right trajectory."

Then the call goes dark. Bram likes a good exit, and my horror-show reflection is burned into the screen.

He has no plan. There is no new trajectory, no getting me to the next level. I cannot expect to hear from him today, nor tonight, and maybe not tomorrow. He'll call when he wants to, whenever the mood hits him.

I sleep through the day again and the night that follows, but it's not really sleep. It's mostly me horizontal staring up at Kenny's floorboards, tracing the light under the front door, blowing at piles of sawdust, rearranging the letters on the spines of piled books. Now and then there's a siren crossing the hillside. At some point, I eat a pudding cup from an EggSprout box. In the middle of the night, I get a draft coming at me, I try to feel where it's coming from. I find it with my finger, a fresh bullet hole in a window. Except I haven't heard any gunfire lately.

When morning comes, I hear my dropped delivery. I feel like I should rush, and when I open it to catch him, he's working through a brownie he's lifted from my boxes, not even trying to avoid getting caught.

"Shit," he says, grinning, crumbs falling on his T-shirt.

"Do you want to come in? Have a coffee, split a pastry? Seems like we're always super rushed."

Lennon swallows hard, not sure what to do here, wiping more crumbs across his shirt. I step back to clear the way, but he doesn't get far, shaking his head, covering his nose while he points at the boxes of spoiled food everywhere. He gags again in the vestibule. But then he turns and grins at me, like I've pulled some sort of prank.

"Okay, okay." I close the door behind me and join him on the landing, watching how he tries to accommodate my knee, stepping back, hovering, ready to grab and steady me. I sit myself on the top step. He slides past me to the one below, my throbbing ugliness perched between us. I dig through the day's boxes and find something easy, a couple of cold sausages. I pass one to him.

"Nice," Lennon says, and we touch links before biting, like a champagne toast to a grand new day. A pause to appreciate that yesterday is over. And a moment to stew on where we're at this morning, with no plan, and no going back, just a bullet lodged someplace I haven't found yet.

Things fall quiet quick. We chew instead of talking. He doesn't ask about my recovery. I don't press him on law school. He has sweat stains down the back of his EggSprout shirt. I probably have the same. I've been wearing the same ripped slacks all week.

The morning dampness is thick, and I have doubts about staying longer, feeling the cold getting under my brace. But we finish pretty quickly, and we get up together, rising in unison. "Really nice," Lennon tells me, and he touches me on the shoulder. Just a soft, simple pat.

"Thank you," I tell him. This is better. This is progress. A bona fide connection, right here on my doorstep. Lennon has delivered a small dose of hope.

"Number 1044," Lennon reads from my standing order. "Have a nice day, 1044."

He doesn't know my name, which just about breaks my heart. He's already up and running, skipping the cartwheels but dashing in zigzags back to his van.

CHAPTER FIFTEEN

I'VE GONE BACK TO bed. Lennon has been exhausting, and no one online is going to perk me up. I could stay here all day, pop the pills I've been skipping, and probably even heal a bit by just checking out. But I smell trouble outside. An overactive fireplace, maybe a trash bin fire; maybe Darrel is down on the curb again. Something toxic is burning not far away. Then a chorus of sirens, and I remember nights with Sylvie. There were times, now and then, when we reached for each other and our breathing would fall in sync across the pillows in the dark.

But the smell is getting stronger, and the sirens are getting louder, and from my bed, through the windows, I can watch a man in a yellow jacket rappel down a neighbor's roof. By the time I cross the room, the intersection is jammed with hoses and ladder trucks. Heavy-clad firefighters are circling the building on the corner opposite Marleen's.

Smoke streams out the windows, black and fast-moving, then spits through the cracks in the eaves. All of it seeps skyward, rising to mix with fog. Finally, as panes start to burst, I begin seeing flames. On the roof, the daredevil firefighter is swinging front to back, dragging along with him a Thor-sized ax. He coaxes a hefty column of smoke through a hole he's just made.

For the next hour or so, it burns everywhere it can, with more flames taking over more rooms in the building. The far side of the structure is hidden from me, but I've seen it before, and I know it when I hear it: a glass penthouse addition, a fancy room framed with windows, a high rooftop perch where someone special gets to sit—the shatter is enormous, a massive waterfall of glitter that first breaks at the roof level, then again on the street. The noise lasts forever, and the crew has to step back. Their boots crunch through glass now as they run back to the flames.

It's a three-story wood frame with two separate units. The top one once enjoyed a penthouse suite. On the lower floors, the shades are always drawn down. Dim lamplight and shadows have been the only signs of life. A lot of buildings across the hill sit the same way, crouched in the fog, easily mistaken for deserted. That's why I don't recognize them, the man, woman, and child watching from the curb. They're attended by a firefighter in a T-shirt with a clipboard. They cringe as flames lunge through another window. They have to look away when it takes out a lower one. A pair of roller bags, duffels, and briefcases are at their feet. An oversized boy is stuffed into a stroller, which they rock back and forth in a quick, manic way.

I've never seen them on the street. They come and go from a garage deep under their house. They keep to themselves, and they keep things status quo, avoiding outlandish upgrades, except for all the windows installed on their roof.

My first thought is to run down and help as I can. Coffee, blankets, making phone calls to relatives, the basics any neighbor would be happy to do. But my knee is still ballooned, and when I try to get up, there's a different, queer numbness. I can't get anywhere. I close my eyes and slip back into my chair.

My next thought is an explosion. Maybe one got out of control. That's the most likely cause, especially once the cops arrive, the same ones who came round to quiz me about Kenny. They jump out of their car and make a beeline for Max and Marleen. The two women are keeping watch, dutiful and worried. As the police approach, Max steps up and puts her hands on their shoulders, first one officer, then the other. As best I can hear, she talks to them the way she talked to me. "Oh, honey," she's telling them, with unfazed authority, before sending them back to their patrol car.

Then Kenny is running down our stairs, charging at his usual pace. He stops at the sidewalk like he's surprised by it all, the fire, the trucks, and the building in flames. He takes it in quick, then looks up and down the street, like he still expects a car to whisk him away. But the officers quickly flank him, escorting him to their vehicle, parked with the fire equipment in the middle of the street.

With the fire really stepping up, raging from all corners, the glass on my windows starts to feel the heat. The smoke goes straight up before it's pushed sideways, far over my head and the wooden lady above me. We have front-row seats. We watch embers float toward us. Several loopy-loop in the breeze before fizzing out on the glass, like an army of angry snowflakes.

I watch Kenny below me, trying to reason with the police. He shakes his head and tries to focus on his phone, until the officers have had enough. They put a hand on Kenny's head and guide him to the backseat. I can almost see him back there, not your average sidewalk perp, in his subtle open collar and pricey selvedge jeans, now talking nonstop to whomever he's calling. They drive Kenny away, leaving more space for pumps and ladders, which skip the sirens now for blinding flashing lights.

The fire builds for another half hour with more holes in the roof and lots of windows getting bashed open. The crew scrambles and circles and, pretty remarkably, they get it contained. It's breathtaking every time—how a fire gets turned down, how they keep it from spreading. The embers act like they're under group hypnosis, the way they fall off together, retreating all at once. The pace slows, and the cloud of ashes thins. I've been sitting here watching, thinking this was the one. This is how it would end, in a pillar of flames right here at my desk.

I expected the hill to be engulfed. I expected the next building, then the next, to catch fire and pass it forward, shoulder to shoulder as we are, crowded together just waiting our turn. I expected it to reduce my home to nothing, By the middle of the day, it'd be as if I never happened. The wooden lady overhead would seem impossible, too.

Across the hill, every blue tarp has its own reason—an exploded pilot light, a cheap holiday candle, a kitchen grease fire at a Passover meal. Each time, I watched for the city's explanations, scrolling my screen on the edge of my seat. But they all end same: neighbors divided into victims and onlookers, even though we're all staring down the same threat.

By the end of the second hour, it looks like an ordinary drill. The main crew moves in methodical choreography, bustling around for the next several hours, double-checking their results. By then, the stream of office workers has diverted its course, a little irked by the trucks and the broken glass, but also flashing quick sympathies when they spot the family left wet and waiting on the sidewalk.

Once the roof is burnt down to a husk, I have a clear view of the upper floors and the piles of debris. It's dripping from every angle, looking ashamed and defeated, like it's lost its final battle. The mess of it sort of exhales, sagging, deflating, reluctantly releasing its last plumes of smoke. Where the floor is still intact, two chairs are left standing, miraculously untouched, or at least un-burnt, their pale yellow upholstery soaked and filthy but starkly alone where everything else has burned off.

The ground floor, a separate family's home, has also been spared. Its bright yellow siding is soiled but still in place. That family isn't hovering. They aren't huddled on their curb. They don't seem to be available at all this morning.

I start limping back and forth between my windows and the vestibule, antsy to get down there, feeling lame and helpless. And then Lennon comes skipping over hoses and puddles, his van probably parked a block or more away.

I hang on my doorframe, holding my knee up, calling him as he bounds up the stairs. "Really wish I could be down there, pitching in somehow."

"Pitching in?" He looks me up and down. "What do you think you could do?" He hands me a box he missed before, a little put off by the effort, only half-smiling through sweat and a squint.

"I'm just saying…if I weren't injured…I'd like to be a good neighbor."

I watch his smile soften, going weak at the edges. Eye to eye now, he looks confused, and the longer we stand here, he's not smiling at all. He's come every day and cheerfully kept himself a stranger. Now, the morning of a close call, with smoldering still going, he looks disgusted and impatient, like I'm the real trouble here, like he's always resented climbing my steps.

Going down, he takes them two at a time, fast as he can. A couple firefighters see him coming and throw up their hands, calling Lennon's name like the party's just starting.

When I check my screen, first reports link the fire to a string of suspicious activities, all of which name Kenny as a prime suspect—the same arrest record I found in my quick search, the warehouse party fire, a link to a petty theft ring and, a new one for me, his vocal opposition to Dr. Aliah Alam. He calls her a "busybody on an international scale," someone who spends twenty-four hours in the city and "thinks she knows how we really live." Reporters suspect Kenny set the fire to frame others, probably people trying to sleep in the park up the hill. Dr. Alam hit a nerve, the transit hub hit it again, and an odd duck like Kenny, who comes off as a crank, is easy to picture doing extreme things.

Out the window, inspectors are getting to work, lingering, going in and out, taking turns in the two yellow exposed chairs. They look up at the sky, pointing at circling hawks, and as dusk comes around, they set up a small network of hooded floodlights. Where blackened framing still stands, wires and pipes are exposed, and from my desk, I watch them until they're taking their dinner, passing foil-wrapped burritos around the charred living room.

On my screen, the local news features Kenny in a live stream from a courthouse downtown. "This should be a wake-up call. More fires are coming, and more people like me will get dragged in like this." He's talking to someone off screen, and he's still in yesterday's clothes, covered in sweat that amplifies his crazed look.

A young man in jeans and a T-shirt swivels his camera phone, moving between close-ups of himself and Kenny's forehead. It's dizzying, but it's all the local news has to work with. "Just to confirm," the kid presses, "did you set your neighbor's building on fire yesterday? Or any others nearby? What about the warehouse party fire? Are you into arson or what?"

The phone swings back to Kenny. "Are you kidding?" He starts walking, trying to shake the kid, changing directions across the courthouse steps.

The kid and his camera keep close, trying to push the same theory I've read about. "Are you ready to blame people in the park encampment? Do you think the fires are all about payback?"

"That's disgusting," Kenny says, pushing at the lens. He had the same irked expression when I fell down the stairs, inconvenienced, frustrated, with bigger things to get to.

I'm not Kenny's biggest fan. He's not much for sweeping sawdust. But here he is getting hassled after getting hauled in for questioning, his name muddied and his home nearly burnt down by embers. The love of his life has to rely on a tin box, and that must mean they're not back in their old bubble. I've never understood why Kenny over-shares with me—but I get I should try to be less irritated. Today in particular, I'm lucky to have anyone sharing at all.

A bright light starts flooding him, from behind the kid interviewer, and Kenny lifts a hand to shield the glare. It's a lighting rig hoisted by professional newscasters, a small group just now arriving on the scene. "What about your opinions on the transit hub, sir?" They lob a few questions, just like the kid. "You've been very vocal about a 'new influx.' Do you think there's a link to the fire at your neighbors'?"

The feed cuts to local anchors behind a desk in a studio. They haven't been listening, and they don't remark on the interview. Instead they read a statement claiming a suspect is in custody, not Kenny at all but a man they won't name, except to say "he has no known address and may or may not live in one of the city's parks." The anchor, a hulking man almost busting his suit seams, takes a moment to shake his head. "Sorry," he says, looking away from the camera. "I don't think it should be worded like that."

By the afternoon, downhill traffic is heavy. A few people have stopped to take postable photos, posing in front of the two yellow chairs. I've been hunting for more news and keeping an eye out for Kenny. I missed the first runners, high schoolers playing hooky in the park up the hill, yelling as they hightail it down to safety. But I look up in time to catch a half-dozen Germans, arms full from a picnic, rented blankets and baskets and boxes of prepared food, shouting at each other as they look over their shoulders, expecting something to come after them, and shrieking again when they see the burnt house.

Sirens follow, and a pair of patrol cars charge up the hill. I wait for fire engines, but they never come. It's another kind of disturbance, a different sort of trouble—maybe a backlash, maybe not.

When Kenny steps out of a car, he looks for me in my window. I take a step back, so I don't think he spots me. He looks haggard, filthy, his collar and jeans not looking so crisp. The fire's smell is still bracing, and the building's burnt husk really commands the street. But I don't think Kenny notices. He's checking his phone on the spot where Darrel burnt his stuff, thumb and fingers moving fast, and while he's still at it, he looks up at the wooden lady and screams Darrel's name.

CHAPTER SIXTEEN

THE SPLEEN, IT TURNS out, is an organ of integrity. It gets rid of the old, brings in the new, and just sort of sticks around to fight off the worst. I try to feel it on my side, somewhere under my arm, but it's buried in there behind too much stuff.

This morning there's a note secured to my door by a wad of chewed gum. "Last day! Leaving town! U should 2! – Lennon from EggSprout." I get what he's thinking. He knows when to clear out.

The building across the street still smells like it's smoldering even though it's not.

The morning dampness is heavy with ash, and when I inhale deep, I get the bitter rip of burnt cooking fuel: a small chemical fire burns in front of the ruined house, where a stranger bends over a can of Sterno.

I should be infuriated. I should be calling the cops. Maybe limp over myself and try to rush him with my brace, But he's just cooking his breakfast, making himself a warm meal. I read earlier the city has already raided the parks.

"Good morning!" I wave. He looks around, spots me, and quickly starts gathering his stuff.

I approach our stairs slowly, respecting the brace now, one leg stuck out like a rusty tin man and one hand never leaving the rail.

The gentleman watches me thump my way down; I watch him backing away as I do. He's grabbed all his things—a backpack, three shopping bags, a bedroll, and the Sterno—before I hit sidewalk level.

"God help us," I hear him say, and he takes off down the street, as if escaping a woken monster, an ogre from a cave. I follow after him, slow and steady, crossing the street and feeling iffy, trying to pull off a painful drag-and-hop maneuver. But otherwise, beyond that, the neighbors' buildings give me balance. I drag my hand along their plaster, and they give me their support. I don't want to end up in Marleen's spare room again. This morning all I want is to see how the new transit hub is coming.

We all heard the explosions, we all weathered the shaking, and we all know how awful the final product will be. The posters in the library basement were very clear. No charm. Void of magic. Master planned with too much concrete. But I'd still like to see how these first days are going. The view from my windows has been giving me nothing; the block between me and the busy commuter corner is lined with trees that never give up their leaves.

The gentleman trailing Sterno is already round the corner, giving a last panicked look. When I clear the trees and reach the same corner, I have to adjust to the sidewalk's grade. I look ahead and face the devastation. It is vast in ways I could never imagine in a crowded library basement.

The intersection is a hive of hellish activity. Buses, trucks, and cars are gridlocked and steaming. Heavy equipment, some of it two stories high, inches its way down the street. They've dug a large, deep pit where a worn-out drugstore and chain grocery used to sit. That's all gone, replaced by a rocky cavity with its own dirt ramp.

The dampness feels thicker here. Construction barricades have squeezed the sidewalk, and once I'm around the corner, I'm shuffled to the side. People push past and are irritated by my slowness.

I don't stay long. I've seen this before—half the city has been excavated and rocky pits are regular features. I don't need to waste time gawking or pining, gobbing up the flow to mourn an old lot.

I have to be careful with all the briefcases and backpacks. Every one of them flies by exactly at knee level. But once I'm back round the corner and headed uphill again, I find my own pace, and I take a short breather, leaning on a tree with gigantic white blossoms.

The shift is remarkable. The rocky pit feels miles away. The tidy stoops and scrubbed stairways, the old cornices and new lamps, the sleek house numbers posted on ancient shingles—and folks have cleaned up here since the fire yesterday. Sidewalks have been swept, driveways are hosed down. It is charming, it is magic, and ahead through the leaves, the painted wooden lady soars above my windows, sticking out several feet beyond the roofline. She looks a little unsteady, wobbling a bit in the breeze. A decent gust could shove her off—a terrifying projectile. Or a busty avenging angel that could descend at any moment.

Then the neighbors' burnt building comes into view. The pair of yellow chairs has already disappeared, maybe with vandals or maybe they melted into the cinders overnight. Right now a small crew is securing a blue tarp, stretching it over the blackened trusses. Also from the corner, another site that's tough to swallow: a new tag in green, another #notwelcome, this time neon bright on my own sidewalk.

I watch a police car pull up and two officers jump out, scrambling up the stairs to our shared vestibule. I can't rush over, and no one seems to notice me, so I use Marleen's building to steady myself. But they just rush down again and wait there on the cub, looking up the front doors just like me.

Kenny emerges slower and more deliberately than I've ever seen him, sort of taking the steps backward in order to guide Darrel behind him. He's a surprise to me. I hadn't thought about Darrel when the building was burning. I never worried he might be just as horrified. He was probably beside himself when Kenny disappeared in the back of a police car. I never even considered he was upstairs, watching all of this too.

I tighten my grip and watch a man and a woman, both with nametags or badges, follow Darrel down the steps and angle him from the back end. Everyone is focused on getting him where he's going, down to street level, and he looks like he's in pain going down the steps. Darrel wears more clothes than the last time I saw him, a sweatshirt and a bomber jacket hiding his heart equipment. He's calmer, too, nodding as he goes—not resisting, not yelling. In fact, no one is talking. The feeling is somber. An exit procession that feels very negotiated.

From across the street, his Mohawk is still beautiful, still aggressive and severe despite his slow movements. At the curb, a white minivan pulls up with perfect timing. Darrel gets helped in. At least I think he's getting helped in. I watch the van pull off and the police car follow after.

"They took him," Kenny tells me as I cross the street. He's at the top of our stairs again. "Social services," he adds when I stop and catch my breath. I grab the rail and nod up at him, taking each step in slow, measured hops. "County facility," he goes on, and even taking it slow, I'm too winded to respond. "He was getting infections. He wouldn't take care of them. The whole procedure is in jeopardy, so they're insisting on psychological oversight."

"Kenny," I tell him. My heavy breathing must be obvious. "I'm sure you did all you could. I know you did."

"I did what I could," Kenny repeats back to me. "I guess I did." He steps aside to make room, but that's about it. Nose to nose now, he's hard to look at. I'm sure I'm the same. He's as sweaty as me. His heart is also pounding. But from the top of the steps, I can see where he's looking, and it's way past me—down the hill and the street to Darrel's caravan, the van and police car speeding off across town. Kenny doesn't have to share more for me to know what Darell's in for. Therapies, psychotropics, surgeries never-ending. Locked-down rehab and ready access to hospice. Institutionalization—extended, probably permanent. The county facility is a prison on a high hill, surrounded by grassy lawns and ocean views.

Once the van rounds the corner, Kenny points at my brace. "Looks like it's mending." But he doesn't mean it. He's not looking, not really, and as I navigate around him, I nod and leave him out there on our front steps.

I cross to my desk and sit down to business, sending Bram a canceled contract and unsubscribing from the queue that belongs to St. Louis. It will be two weeks before I can rely on my knee again, but I cancel my standing order with EggSprout right away regardless. Months later, I learn that they've gone out of business, and I see photos, maybe doctored, of multiple EggSprout vans driven off a pier and left piled up in shallow bay waters.

Nowadays I walk several blocks past the hub construction to a corner market with vegetables, run by a pleasant family from Managua. I'm happy to be out more, happy to be off the pills, happy to have the brace stored under the bed. I only look at my screen once or twice a day now. I check messages when I have to. I've bought curtains for the windows, sheer ones that let the light in.

Not long ago, a small explosion went off across the street. Just like I'd heard before. I looked up in time to see Marleen's building shake a little.

I stood at the window and saw Marleen at hers. She was raising the blinds, then lifting the panes, trying to get some fresh air circulating through. It was the bedroom I was in, except filled with smoke, the slow-moving, billowy kind, with not much force to it, but a lot of it, voluminous. It headed out the open windows, where it climbed like creepy fingers up the side and over the roof.

Marleen waved her arms to help clear the space. Then she waved over at me. Not in a friendly way. More like a signal.

"You're not the neighbors we expected," she shouted over to me. I shrugged, and she coughed as the smoke passed between us.

When the air finally cleared, I saw the room behind her, and a stroller, a fancy one, parked inside the window. I hadn't seen it wheeled in; they were keeping the blind pulled, and no one had been round with an update. But I was sure that's what it was. Surrounded by furniture delivery boxes.

"What the hell are you doing?" I shouted then.

"Getting the nursery set up."

"But I keep hearing explosions…"

She leaned out the window, like she couldn't possibly hear me because Max and Sylvie were coming in just then, laughing and talking, lifting glasses between them, bringing another for her and insisting she match them. When Sylvie joined Marleen at the window, she spotted me sitting in mine, and without a wave or a wink, not a gesture of any kind, she moved from window to window and pulled the blinds down.

Upstairs, above me, there's a new kind of commotion. It's not the arguing I used to hear or angry pounding down the steps. It's Kenny and his new friends, frequent fresh visitors playing music and laughing loud. I've watched them arrive in cars and taxis, a messy crowd that skews young and looks a little rough. They don't look like office workers. I doubt they're Kenny's foundation staff. But the music bumps up like never before, and for a while, when it first starts, Darrel's sawdust fell down here like a fierce, steady storm.

That's when I order sheetrock for the walls and the ceiling. I bring in professionals to install it, and I leave them alone, vacating to coffee shops and giving my knee extra workouts that really help. When they finish, it looks right, like it should've when I started: a long open sweep where the light doesn't stop—but with proper walls, the plumbing concealed and wires hidden in ways that aren't such a fire hazard. I move the desk from the window and slide the couch in its place. The low-slung chair fits nicely beside it.

I often sit there quietly. Some mornings, I just sit and listen to my breath. I have given up on work, relying instead on Sylvie's trust and, as planned, funneling the dog calendars' profits to St. Louis and Kate. I hope they've stepped up their plans. I hope the spleen makes every shortlist. I hope the world is changed by a new look at our insides, the reasons and explanations why everything works.

A few projects I still wish we could've done together: a novel of fires, massive cleansing fires, fires that decimate families and level whole communities; a history of libraries, specifically local libraries, more specifically the forces that fill cookie buffets; a hybrid design sketch on the impact of subways and the psychological effects of going down to go forward; an investigation into the ecosystem of books, wherein they're talked about more but actually read less with the cost-benefit of evolving to a purely decorative place. And also this one: an illustrated book of mythical missing figureheads, with drawings of the voyagers who rescued them and sketches of the ones still lost in the deep.

Another hurdle for St. Louis: Kate jumped ship once she heard about Bram. She transitioned fast, made the jump with some fanfare, landing as the editor/chief provocateur at an esteemed review journal. In her new post, she teased about flatness and the science behind flatness, and in her inaugural essay, without naming names, she wished me well but hoped that I walk off the edge of the earth. In the next paragraphs, she praised the contributors featured in her first issue, noting a study of the physics against three dimensions, a lyrical ode to wishful thinking, and short speculative fiction on dogs' role in history. I appreciate her self-confidence and the strength others see in her. I don't care now about the attention she used to throw my way.

The other day, I saw the woman from the library basement, the one ready with a shove and neon spray paint. I was sitting in the window, my eyes closed for a bit, just feeling the sun on my face and on my neck. When I opened them, I saw her watching me from below, market bags in both hands. I started to gesture, but she closed her eyes and stood there the same way, just feeling the sun warm against her skin.

Not long ago, Beau Bram sent me a ticket to Kabul, for a conference where he thought we could meet and travel and I don't know what else. The latest videos I saw of him, he was in a theater in Paris, talking in French, yelling and shouting, the crowd enraptured and a global fashion/luxury brand projected on screens encircling him. He had shaved his head—his beautiful hair totally gone—and he was dressed very simply in a tailored but plain T-shirt and plain tapered jeans. His ranting had become a shtick, a gag people came for, putting down good money to watch a respected author get out of his chair and tear his audience to bits. On the bill, he was expected to talk about people on the margins, the gay book scene in London, and how we see the world through our most intimate relationships. The whole thing looked a lot like a self-help happening, like a workshop encounter that would quickly become a showcase for his rage. There was no specific book he was hawking. No advance purchase or reading required. But he's been filling a lot of auditoriums. After Paris, he sold out Frankfurt, Copenhagen, and a large ornate hall in Rome. Just before he was scheduled to arrive in Kabul, an attack and explosion closed the hotel where he'd arranged for us stay. I saw photos of the carnage, guests and locals laid out side by side on the curb. Dr. Alam showed up on some TV coverage, offering her commentary, dispassionate and direct about how horrible things are.

When I look out my windows now, I see blue tarps tight and firm, resisting the fog and the damp heavy winds. It's a very gray morning, not so unusual, everyone tucked into scarves and wool coats. This morning, across the hill, I see smoke rising in a single thick plume from a tiny attic window several blocks away. The building is four stories tall, a magnificent painted lady busting out over the hill with a column of rounded windows that have stood there forever—since the time the whole city shook and burned down. It's covered in vermillion, cobalt, and turquoise, with small golden balls and a steeply pitched roof.

The sirens start up. The air begins to thicken. The smoke and the embers start heading this way. The building is tucked into a row of tall ladies, with small arches and peaks and strange curlicues. On the street above it, another plume is rising from what looks like a barn, red and white under a black gambrel roof, with two slopes on each side, one shallow, one steep. Not so far away, a big, thick apartment looks borrowed from Chinatown, done up in glossy blacks, shiny reds, and greens from peacocks. That one already has flames out its windows. More sirens join in, then car horns start up, and a half dozen people are charging up the sidewalk. Across the hill, old and new press closer than ever, leaning into one another. And as the wind shifts, the smoke gathers, beginning its march toward my five windows.